MW01146929

# A Killer's Game

## A Detective Lenny Shane Novel

## Amy Andrews

Copyright © 2014 Amy Andrews
All rights reserved
ISBN-13: 978-1500569457
Printed by Createspace

# DEDICATION
This book is dedicated in loving memory
of my Dad. I miss you everyday.

# CONTENTS

# ACKNOWLEDGMENTS

I would like to thank James @ GoOnWrite, for designing a beautiful cover. I would like to give a special thanks to Andrew, for always being there to help me bounce my ideas around. Thank you! I love you! Your input helped me more than you know! I would also like to thank my Mom, Christina, for her endless encouragement and support! And lastly, I would like to thank my kitty, Oreo, for always wanting to snuggle, when Mommy really needs to be typing. LOL!

# 1 THE ESCAPE PLAN

ANXIOUSLY waiting for the sound of the buzzer, Robert Verde paced back and forth, like a caged animal, with his hands fidgeting in front of him. His soft soled shoes barely made a sound on the concrete floor, in his tiny six by eight cell. Holding his eyes closed, his lips moved in an inaudible silence, as he obsessively reviewed his escape plan. This was it. It was now or never. The moment he had been waiting and planning for, was nearly here. Tonight was the night. When the buzzer sounded, and the barred door slid open, it was going to be lights, camera, action!

Having nothing but time on his hands to plan every detail he could think of, he had every confidence that his planned escape from the Miami Dade Correctional Facility would go flawlessly, and be executed with nothing less than perfection. He had even made several dry runs within the prison walls over the past couple of weeks.

One always had to be prepared for unforeseen circumstances, though. Knowing and realizing this, even through his confidence, Verde stopped pacing, and took three strides, over to his three inch thick twin sized mattress. Lifting it up, he fished his fingers into the barely visible one inch incision he had made into it sometime earlier, and pulled out a small, sharp object. Rolling the plastic handle between his fingers, he admired his craftsmanship, as the light gleamed off of the blade. It was a crude tool, made with the blade of a shaving razor, the handle of a toothbrush, and a bic lighter, but it would be effective. Verde chuckled to himself at how resourceful and creative one could become, when given no other choice. He took the object and tucked it carefully into his white, calf-high sock, right next to the photograph of his little Bobby, that had once adorned his cell wall, right above his bed.

Wanting to make his escape as quietly and as unnoticed as possible, he hoped that he did not have to make a mess of things by having to use the blade, but he would use it if it came down to it. Nothing made him feel more alive than the feel of the blade penetrating soft flesh. Watching the eyes turn into a milky stillness. He had killed many times before, and quite enjoyed it. That is what landed him in this hellish compound.

Prisoners like him had nothing to lose. He was already on death row with no possibility for parole, thanks to that relentless Detective Lenny Shane. What is the worst that could happen? Death, while trying to escape? Ha! At least he would die with his dignity, and he would die trying.

The buzzer sounded, and his caged cell door clicked open. Verde shot out of the cell, like a racehorse at the Kentucky Derby. Any other night, he would have taken his sweet time, because it gave him more time out of his confined quarters. Tonight, his black crocks could barely keep up with his fast moving feet, as they strode quickly over the painted concrete, past the rows of cell doors. Like an expertly launched pinball, he maneuvered swiftly to the left and to the right, in between and around the other inmates, without ever breaking his stride.

It was six o'clock in the evening, which meant chow time. Verde's stomach knotted and growled audibly, because it knew what time it was as well. Too bad. His stomach would have to wait, because it wasn't going to get fed dinner at it's usual time. Not tonight. As with all other evenings, before going to the dining hall, he had to report to the medical wing, for his nightly cocktail of psychiatric meds. He could skip dinner without being noticed, but he couldn't miss showing up for his meds. The sirens would whale, and the guards would lock the prison down for a head count, until he was found. This needed to be avoided in order to give him a three hour window until lights out, which is when the next scheduled head count was.

He didn't need the meds, and he didn't like them. When he did take them, they put him in a zombie like state of submission. He had perfected the art of sleight of hand, enabling him to fool the nursing staff into thinking he had taken them. He made the entire scheme plausible by enacting the trance like stupor the meds would have put him in, had he actually taken them. He often thought he should be awarded an Oscar for his superior acting skills. If there was a Golden Globe or some other prestigious award for prisoners, he would definitely take home the trophy.

Verde stood behind two other inmates in the single file line, with his arms down at his sides, tapping and rolling his fingers on his thighs. Bumping shoulders with the inmate that was coming out of the med room, the plump Nurse Betty said in her sweet southern drawl, "My, my, my, Robert. We're in a hurry tonight, aren't we?"

A faint smile crossed his lips. When he saw Nurse Betty, it was the only time he was referred to by his first name. Usually it was by his inmate number, 184129, or his last name. She reminded him of his sweet Grandmother, with her loosely curled silver hair, withered red lips, and her Southern disposition. Rest her soul. She was the woman who raised him from the age of twelve. A good woman, unlike his crack-head slut egg donor…and the woman with whom he had a child. He guessed it was true what they said about marrying someone like your Mother, because he had. Took off like his Mother too. But, the system awarded his Grandmother custody a little too late. The emotional damage had already been done.

"Just real hungry tonight, Nurse Betty. Anxious to get to the dining room, I guess."

"Well, if you're a good boy, like always, Nurse Betty might have a treat for you," she said in a whisper.

Verde accepted his pill filled paper Dixie cup, and another filled with water. Throwing his head back, he opened wide, and took the pills into his mouth. Tasting the bitterness of the chalky pills starting to dissolve, he stuck his tongue out to show Nurse Betty. Immediately bringing the second cup to his mouth, with a flick of his tongue, Verde spit the pills into the water, and drank it, filtering the pills out with his teeth. He dramatically swallowed hard. When the last bit of water was swallowed, Verde crumpled both cups, and tossed them into the garbage. Bending over to Nurse Betty's eye level, he opened his mouth wide, and moved his tongue around, up and down, side to side. It was nowhere near a Criss Angel caliber illusion, but it worked. Especially with the senile nursing staff. Because he liked her, he felt a small pang of guilt for deceiving her, but he could live with it. It was definitely better than the alternative.

Pleased with him, Nurse Betty said, "now, that's a good boy." Reaching into her dark blue scrubs pocket, she fetched out a snickers bar. Handing it to him, she gave him a wink.

Verde took the candy bar, and nestled it in between his chest and the white tank top he was wearing beneath his uniform. Walking out the door, he stopped in the middle of the door frame, turned around, and said, "thanks, Nurse Betty."

Nurse Betty's red colored, puckered lips just smiled and said, "well, you're quite welcome, sweetie… Thank you." She liked him because she had been employed their since his first day as an inmate. He never gave her any trouble, unlike some of the others.

Verde studied her face for a moment in silence, then simply turned and continued walking out the door, back into the hallway. His pace slowed to normal, as he didn't want to stand out to the guard. Slipping back into the end of the line, Verde went unnoticed in the sea of standard issued orange jumpsuits.

Keeping himself tucked close to the wall, Verde peered over the shoulder of the guy in front of him.

The guard stood near the entrance to the med wing at the front of the line. Verde's eyes were trained on the him, watching his every move, or lack of it.

The silent stillness of the inmates standing in line, was disturbed when a loud commotion came from within the medical room.

"I ain't takin' that fuckin' shit," a booming redneck voice said, followed by the sound of Nurse Betty's metal tray clattering onto the concrete floor.

The line of inmates broke out into cheers, hoots, and hollers, spurring on the insubordination of their fellow inmate.

If he hadn't had alternate plans this evening, Verde would have waited to see whom it was that was giving Nurse Betty guff. He would have nipped that problem right in the bud. Or, shanked it right in the gut.

Whatever. Tonight, it was a perfectly timed distraction that he intended to take full advantage of, and he would just have to let the staff handle it, like they always did.

Verde watched until the guard's back disappeared into the medical room, to get the situation under control, either with their billy clubs, pepper spray, or stun guns. Spinning around, he kept himself tucked against the wall, as he crept as silently and as quickly as a ninja, away from the line of inmates.

Looking over his shoulder, Verde picked up the pace. He had to get around the corner before the guard stepped back out into the hallway.

Verde slithered around the corner, and stood with his back against the wall. Slowly, he poked his head around, to take a peek back around the corner. The guard was still not back to his post.

Removing his shoes, he held them in one hand. With only his socks on his feet, he tilted his neck back and watched the video camera that was mounted on the wall directly above his head. It was scanning the length of the hallway, and was nearly back to his end. If he timed it perfectly, he could outrun the camera, and not be seen. The camera body panned to perfect vertical position from Verde's view. His socks didn't offer much traction, as he took off in a dead sprint. Keeping his eyes trained on the set of double doors, at the end of the long corridor, Verde watched for movement, through the two thick glass panels on each of the steel doors, while his feet moved as fast as his eyes did.

Sliding on his socks for the last eight feet or so, Verde whipped his head back around, and his eyes darted to the camera at the opposite end of the hall. Having just seconds before the camera's lens reached his exact spot, he gingerly pushed the long metal bar that ran the width of the door. He opened the door only wide enough for him to slide through to the other side. Now on the other side of the door, Verde immediately squatted below the sight line of the glass, to avoid being detected by the camera. Holding his breath, his heart pumped hard with adrenaline, as the doors clicked shut. He hoped that the continuing commotion in the hallway was enough to mask the sound. After silently counting to five in his head, he slipped his crocks back on, and moved double time, down the last corridor. He was heading towards the laundry facility, and had fifteen more minutes until the nightly pick up. He knew this place like the back of his hand, and was careful to time and avoid all of the cameras, as well as any guards roaming the halls.

Entering the laundry facility, through two more sets of steel double doors, Verde recognized the two young male workers. Each of them were filling large wheeled bins with soiled linens, then rolling them to the front of the warehouse, near the large bay pick up door. This included everything from bedding, to towels and washcloths, to aprons used by the kitchen staff.

Glancing around, Verde saw the specific bins of laundry he was looking for. The ones filled with the prisoner's custom orange jumpsuits. There were about six large bins filled with the uniforms. They were sitting off to the side, at the rear of the warehouse.

The two workers were currently occupied with moving the bins full of the dingy white, soiled prisoner bedding.

Sneaking behind bin to bin, Verde concealed his presence until he reached the bright orange cotton filled bins. Ducking low, and peering from around them, he watched intently.

This was going to be even easier than he thought. The two workers each had blaring headphones on, and were not really paying much attention to their surroundings.

While neither one was looking, Verde grasped the rails of one of the carts, bent his knees, and heaved himself up and over. He somersaulted into the cart, causing it's wheels to roll slightly from the force.

Verde quickly started tunneling through the linens, covering and burying himself deeper into the cart.

Hearing the music from the blaring headphones approaching, Verde stilled. He was nearly to the bottom of the pile, but not completely. It was stuffy underneath all of the clothing, and Verde crinkled his nose at the grotesque smell of a thousand sweaty men.

The sound of the squeaky laundry cart wheels echoed in the concrete room as it started to roll, and Verde's tension started to ease. He could nearly taste his freedom now, so he relaxed and enjoyed the short ride to the front of the bay. He heard the bay door open, and a *beep, beep, beep* signal, that indicated a large truck backing up.

The truck came to rest, and the engine was cut. Verde heard the driver exit the vehicle, and open the trailer door.

"Load 'em up, boys," the driver said.

Verde heard one of the men say, "you do those ones, and I'll check these ones."

*Shit*, Verde thought, because he knew what this meant. Anytime laundry, or garbage exited the prison, the workers were supposed to take long metal pipes that had a sharp pointed end, and ram it into the pile, to find, but more likely to deter escape attempts. He had snuck down here to observe these two several times, especially over the past couple of weeks, and they didn't always perform all of the tasks their job required. Of all nights, of course tonight they would decide to follow protocol. If he were to get stuck with it in the wrong place, it could prove to be fatal.

Verde scrambled to get into one corner of the bin. It was not an easy task, when he had to tunnel himself through the heap of clothes without too much noticeable disturbance. Reaching an outer corner, he sat motionless. Pressing his head against the side of the bin, with his knees tightly pulled in, he made himself as small as possible. He was not a religious man, but started praying that they would avoid prodding the corners all together.

He heard the men stabbing about the other bins, followed by an, "All clear." Then he would hear the sound of the wheels turning, as the bins were one by one, wheeled up the ramp, into the back of the truck.

He felt his cart shift. Sounds of the stabbing rod probing around him, made his heart beat so fast, he wondered if they might hear it. Clamping his hand over his own mouth, his eyes grew wide in his sea of orange, and he froze.

His abdominal muscles twisted, and his hand muffled the small grunt that escaped his lips. His right calf seared with a hot flash of pain. He only hoped that the worker didn't notice any blood dripping off of the end of the metal post. For several more seconds, that seemed like hours, the prodder was probed around, coming dangerously close to him.

At the moment he heard an, "all clear," he grew limp, as all of the stress and tension dissipated from within him. His body shifted into a reclining position, as the cart he was in was wheeled up the forty-five degree incline, and came to rest in the back of the truck. After hearing several more "all clears," followed by more carts being wheeled into the truck, he heard the rolling metal door on the back of the truck closing. It was like sweet music to his ears.

He would not move a muscle, until he heard the truck exit beyond the prison's gates.

The truck moved briefly, and then came to a halt. Idling motionless for a good two minutes, he knew that the guard at the gate was checking the undercarriage of the vehicle. Finally, he heard the faint sound of the gates opening over the sound of the truck's loud diesel motor. The truck started rolling and picking up speed.

Like a jack-in-the-box, Verde sprung out of the cart, and drew deep breaths of clean air, tinged with diesel fumes. He knew he would have to burrow back in for the second part of his escape. Pulling up his right leg, he saw that the damage was not too bad. It was still bleeding, but it wasn't deep enough to require stitches. He rooted around the other bins until he found a kitchen towel. He wrapped the towel around his wound, and tied it. He didn't make it tight like a tourniquet, just tight enough to stay put, and soak up the blood.

Verde stretched out in a reclining position, on top of his bin, and made himself comfortable for the forty five minute ride. His stomach ceased growling after his taste buds were delighted with the chocolate, peanut, caramel, and nougat goodness of the Snickers bar, compliments of Nurse Betty. Coming to a stop, and hearing the back up signal of the truck, Verde blended back into the bottom of the pile, like a chameleon. He was rolled out of the truck, and into another large warehouse. Hearing the driver was occupied with unloading the rest of the bins, Verde carefully poked his head out to take a look around. The warehouse structure was very noisy with it's industrial sized washing machines, presses, and driers. That was good. He needn't worry about being quiet.

Verde's eyes lit up, as he spied something good. Something very good, indeed. Several large bins that had the words "Goodwill" printed in large blue lettering. *Perfect.* Still in the cart, he made quick work of stripping out of the jumpsuit. Down to his underclothes, he kept an intense watch on the driver, until he was making his way back to the truck to unload more bins. Just when the time was right, Verde catapulted out of his bin, like a cat, and ran across the warehouse, in his boxers, tank top, white socks, and black crocks. He positioned himself behind the Goodwill bins. Rooting around the bin when the driver wasn't looking, he was able to find a pair of faded jeans, a plain blue t-shirt, and a red baseball cap. He made quick work of getting dressed in his free new outfit.

"Fuckin'-a," he whispered, as he came out from behind the bin. With his head held high, he walked right up to the driver as if he belonged there, and asked, "hey man, you gotta smoke I can bum?"

Reaching into his sleeveless flannel shirt pocket, the driver said, "sure," as he handed Verde a Marlboro and offered him a light.

Verde took a deep drag and exhaled, blowing billowing smoke into the wind. "Thanks, man. I'm gonna go on a break. You have yourself a good night," he said as he tipped his hat to the driver, and walked right out the door, and into the busy, lit up nocturnal streets of Miami.

# 2 NIGHT OUT

A HUNDRED miles away from Miami, on the opposite coast of Florida, The Naples Homicide Division sat atop their bare back barstools, at a long and glossy, thickly shellacked high-top table near the stage, in the neon lit sports bar. The table was littered with drinks and appetizers, ranging from chips and salsa to crab cakes. It was a Thursday night, but they were there to support one of their own.

Detective Ethan Layne played lead guitar in his local rock band, *Epitome*. They were a largely popular band, that played classic to modern heavy rock tunes. If not for his addiction to the thrill of his day job, Layne would play full time. It was what he loved to do, and he had a guitar in his hands ever since he could remember. He certainly looked more like a rock star, than a homicide detective. Of the six members of the Division, two of them looked as if they didn't really belong in the seedy bar environment. Layne's partner, Detective Brian Wilshire, was dressed as usual in a suave designer suit with his perfectly coiffed dark blonde hair, that would be better suited sipping his fine cognac in the Ritz Carlton lobby bar. Lieutenant Sara Whitten, well, she looked like she belonged in a library, or a court room. She was beautiful, but stern looking with her jet black tailored business suit, white collard button down shirt, and her auburn hair pulled tightly back, and piled atop her head. The glass of Chardonnay in her hand completed the look. The only thing she was missing was a pair of spectacles hanging around her neck by a thin metal chain. Those that knew her, however, were not fooled by her looks. She was a tough cookie underneath her demure exterior.

Detective Lenny Shane had the most seniority on the team, as Lead Detective, and sat there pitching back a bottle from his half empty bucket of Bud, while he and the newest recruit, Detective Kate Leopold, talked intently over the blaring juke box music. He had been offered the Lieutenant position some years ago, but declined. He wasn't the paper pushing, monkey suit, politically correct for news briefings kind of guy. He belonged out in the field. Detective Lenny Shane's partner, Detective Bobby Thorne, sat at the end of the table, keeping to himself, and his whiskey on the rocks.

As they took their positions on the stage, the four man band was a diverse looking group, between eighties hair band, alternative grunge rock, and punk rock. The crowd broke into a cheer, as the overhead lighting dimmed, and the stage lights cast an eerie glow on the band. They opened their first set with a bang, by playing Metallica's "Seek and Destroy."

While the rest of the team watched Layne manipulate his Schecter guitar with awe, and talked amongst themselves, Thorne bobbed his head to the beat, and sang along with the lyrics like it was his own personal mantra. He wasn't really that into watching the band, but he did like listening to them. He was more into people watching. He particularly liked to watch and observe people he knew. Their body language often said a lot. He sat there through the entire first set, sipping on his whiskey, and inconspicuously watched the members of his team interact with each other.

For instance, he could tell that Layne and Leopold had the hots for each other by the way they kept looking at each other, and glancing away when the other one noticed. He could also tell that Detective Shane was like a very protective Father figure to Detective Leopold, by the way he kept giving the evil eye to any guy that looked her way that didn't meet Daddy's approval.

At the end of the first set, the band took a twenty minute break. Detective Layne approached the table where his fellow comrades were seated. "Hey guys," he said cheerfully, "thanks for coming out."

His partner, Detective Wilshire offered up a fist bump. "Fucking awesome, man! You guys rock!"

Detective Layne smiled, "thanks man."

"Lieutenant," Detective Layne said, acknowledging his boss, Sara Whitten, giving her a wink.

"Detective," she reputed, as she smiled and raised her Chardonnay glass to him.

Layne walked past Thorne, behind and in between Shane and Leopold, giving them a hug. Looking at Shane, Layne joshed, "it's not too loud for you is it, old man?"

Shane narrowed his dark chocolate eyes at Layne and smirked as he fired back in a humorous tone, "Old man or not, I can still take your ass, you long haired hippie. And no, it's not too loud." Shane followed his statement with a nice long chug of his ice cold bottle of beer.

"Who's calling who a long haired hippie," Layne joked, as he gave Lenny's shoulder length salt and pepper pony tail a light tug.

Lenny just rolled his eyes, and laughed. Pulling a Bud out of his bucket, he popped the top off and handed it to Layne.

Still keeping his arm around Leopold, Layne planted a quick peck on her cheek, and gave her shoulder a light squeeze. "I hope you stick around until after the next set," he whispered to her, then walked back towards the stage, giving Thorne a slightly harder than friendly pat on the back as he walked by. He had wanted to get with her from the first moment he saw her as a rookie at their Headquarters, or (HQ). He figured two years was long enough to pine. He needed to man up, and go after what he wanted, or he would never get it.

Kate Leopold was caught completely off guard by the searing heat that radiated out from her core. She sat there completely befuddled, and couldn't speak a word. Layne, interested in her? Maybe she was just reading something into it that was not there. Didn't matter anyway. It would take all of her willpower to stay away from him, if that turned out to be the case, but now was not the time. She just got her Detective shield. Mixing business with pleasure didn't seem like a good idea at this point in time. Maybe after she got a little more time in.

Shane leaned over to Leopold and said, "he's a good catch, that one," nodding in the direction of Detective Ethan Layne.

Leopold's olive skin blushed and said, "and why would you be telling me that?"

"Just in case you were wondering," he said.

Leopold took a long swallow of Bud, and looked at Shane, trying to be completely believable, and said, "well, thanks for the 411, but I wasn't. Wondering, that is."

Shane smiled and tipped his Bud in a toast and said sarcastically, "yeah, okay." He was a Detective, with a lot of years under his belt. He didn't know who she thought she was fooling, but he could read right through the bullshit.

Detectives Shane, Wilshire, and Lieutenant Whitten stayed through the end of the second set, then left for the evening. Detectives Leopold and Thorne stuck around, moving in closer to each other, from opposite ends of the table.

While Leopold had sensed a bit of unease between the rest of the team and Thorne, she couldn't figure out why. He was perfectly nice to her. Charming, even. Maybe it was something that happened between them before she joined the team? She didn't want to pry, so she didn't ask.

While Layne and the rest of the band continued entertaining the crowd, Thorne and Leopold made fun, light, casual conversation. Leopold actually quite enjoyed his company. She didn't like the way it made her feel guilty, with Layne glaring at them. More so directed at Thorne, than her.

Thorne pulled his phone out of his pocket, and Leopold saw that he had two missed calls.

"Hey," he said to Leopold in an elevated voice, placing his hand on her shoulder. "You stay here, I gotta go return a phone call real quick," He excused himself, and Leopold watched as he went outside,

Turning her attention to the entertainment, Leopold noticed Layne smirk, as if in victory, because he must have thought Thorne had left for the night. Leopold returned a shy grin to Layne's wide smile.

Watching and admiring Layne's talent, she didn't even have to look back to know that Thorne had re-entered the bar. She saw it in Layne's face, as his smile disappeared, and his eyes threw daggers. Thorne approached Leopold at the table, but did not take a seat. Layne took a break from banging his long dark hair around, to watch them. He could see that they were in deep discussion about something. Layne wanted to know what it was about, so he signaled his lead singer, Corey, with a nod of his head, for a quick five minute break after they finished their current song.

The band finished the song, and Layne approached the table as Leopold was gathering her things and paying her tab.

"Where you guys going," Layne asked, while gently placing his hand on Leopold's wrist, trying to keep her there with him.

Thorne glanced down at the gesture, raised his eyebrows, and spoke up, "I got a call from the Lieutenant. Apparently, there's a state wide BOLO for an escaped convict from Miami -Dade. They need all available personnel, even the Homicide Division, so Leopold and I have to leave. Now. The Lieutenant, Shane, and Wilshire are already headed to the station for a briefing. The Lieutenant knows that you can't leave right now, but she said to tell you to go home after the gig, get some sleep, and report for duty first thing in the morning."

Layne sighed deep. "Fuck," he grunted, as he rubbed the back of his neck. Not even acknowledging Thorne's presence, he released Leopold's wrist, and said, "Be careful out there, Leopold."

"Always," she responded.

Layne got back up on the stage for the remainder of the fourth set. This gig couldn't get over fast enough. He loved playing music, but if his team needed him, he needed to be there.

As the band started their next song, Layne watched Thorne and Leopold walk out into the night, with a defeated sinking feeling in the pit of his stomach; although, he couldn't quite figure out why.

# 3 THE STRUGGLE

EXITING the bar, Detective Bobby Thorne offered to drive, because he didn't want to ride in Detective Leopold's bright red smart car. He thought the things looked like a roller skate with wheels, on steroids. Not to mention the fact, that cramming his six foot plus frame inside of it, would be like cramming your foot in a shoe that is three times too small.

Leopold turned to Thorne. "So, do you want to just follow me back to my place, so I can drop my car off and ride into the station with you? I don't want to leave my car here, and it's on the way."

"That won't be a problem," he said.

"Okay then," Leopold said, abruptly making a bee line for her little red roller skate.

Thorne jumped into the driver's seat of his Hunter

Green Jeep Cherokee, and sat there with fuming thoughts running through his head, while he was waiting for Leopold to put it in reverse, and get going.

Now that he had a few moments alone, and didn't need to keep up the rouse, he could allow his Mr. Hyde to come out. First of all, he really didn't like to be social, but in order to keep up appearances, he attended this function tonight. It just wouldn't look right in the eyes of the rest of the team, if he didn't. Normalcy, and fitting in were crucial.

Although he wasn't buddy-buddy with anyone on the team, the one person that he knew had a problem with him, was Layne. Detective Layne really had it out for him, and had no qualms about displaying his dislike or distrust, which couldn't have been made more obvious tonight, unless he were to put a flashing neon sign on his head.

Thorne never gave Layne a solid cause for his feelings, but Thorne had to admit to himself, that they were not unfounded. He would give Detective Layne props for that. Maybe Layne just had that natural gut cop instinct, and could see through his charade. He once overheard Layne telling his own partner, Detective Lenny Shane, to "watch his back, because there was something about the guy he didn't like." Maybe it was just because he thought he was after "his girl." Good cop.

Regardless, he had been working and planning too long, and too hard to have someone fuck it up now. Whether Detective Layne was on to him or not, he was forging full speed ahead. Besides, Detective Layne was otherwise occupied at the moment, and he didn't have the time to afford the distraction from his plan. From his real target. The one whose heart he wanted to rip out. Figuratively. Well, literally too, but that would just be too merciful, so he would settle for figuratively.

His partner, Detective Lenny Shane, was the one he was after. Observing the team and their out of office relationships tonight made him giddy. An evil grin spread across his face at the thought of getting a two for one. Let's see how both Detectives Shane and Layne like his next move. A feeling of satisfaction spread through him, as he turned the ignition key, and followed the little red smart car.

#

Back at HQ, Lieutenant Sara Whitten briefed the entire team, except for Detective Layne, who was still playing at the bar.

Handing out a photo and description of the escaped convict to each of the Detectives, she said, "As we've already discussed, we are each going to split up into each of the territories I gave you, and patrol those. If you see the suspect, call it in, and approach with caution. We do not know if he is armed. Leopold," she said, turning to face the newly shielded Detective Kate Leopold, "I want you to tag along with Detective Thorne. I'm not comfortable sending you out alone just yet."

This elicited an eyebrow raise from both Detectives Shane and Wilshire. Lieutenant Whitten, cocked her head at them and said, "Detectives? Do you have a problem with the orders I've given?"

Turning slowly back towards the Lieutenant, Detective Lenny Shane said in his deep, gruff voice. "I am Lead Detective, Lieutenant…Detective Leopold could come with me?"

The Lieutenant thought about it for a minute, and tapped her finger on the photo she held. "Detective Shane, I know you recognize the man in the photo. Do you really think it's a good idea for Leopold to be tagging along with you?"

Detective Shane looked down at the white glossy floor and drew a deep sigh. He did recognize the man in the photo, but he wasn't the only one in the room who did. He was looking at Robert Verde, serial killer. It was one of his first big arrests on the force nearly twenty years ago. Looking down at the photo, Lenny saw that Verde had the same soulless look in his gray eyes, as he did way back then.

His hair had turned from dark brown to a salt and pepper color, but it was the same guy. His face just had more lines and wrinkles now.

Recognizing the insinuation in his Lieutenant's voice, Detective Shane ran his hand over his thick salt and pepper mustache, and said, "no problem with the orders, Lieutenant." Grabbing a piece of Wrigley's gum out of his shirt pocket, Detective Shane popped it into his mouth, and chewed aggressively on it.

Even though Detective Thorne was his partner, Detective Shane didn't trust him completely. Something was just…off about the guy. He couldn't quite put his finger on it, but it was a feeling he couldn't ignore. He never let on to anyone about this feeling, always keeping it professional. Years of being a Detective taught him that a feeling was just a feeling. It wasn't evidence. Until he had something to back up his gut, he would just keep his mouth shut, unless he wanted to get a date with an internal affairs hot shot. Besides, if you were onto someone, it was always best not to let them know about it. If they think no one is looking, that's when they tend to get sloppy and make mistakes. Mistakes that land you in prison, like Robert Verde, serial killer of young women.

"Good," the Lieutenant said. "I want you all back here tomorrow morning. Drink some coffee or some energy drinks, or something, because we will all be pulling all nighters." Dismissing them with a wave of her hand, the team filed out of the briefing room, and out into their vehicles to start their area canvas search for the escaped convict.

#

Thorne and Leopold jumped into his Jeep Grand
Cherokee, where Thorne carefully placed the
photograph on the center console, where he could
admire it.

A wrap on the Jeep window made both Thorne and
Leopold jump. It was Shane, motioning for the
window to be rolled down. *What the hell does he want
now*, Thorne thought. Forcing a smile on his face, he
rolled down the window.

Bending down, Shane peered into the Jeep. Looking
past Thorne, directly at Leopold, he said, "I just
wanted to say, 'be careful out there, kid.'"

"Thank you, I will."

"And you," Shane directed to Thorne, "you better
keep her safe." It wasn't a request, more like a threat.
"That's all. You can go," he said, as he motioned them
on.

Pulling out of the precinct, they headed South on
US41. Reaching the intersection of US41 and Collier
Boulevard, they continued heading South. There were
only a couple of ways that someone coming from
Miami could get to Naples, and this was one of them.
Although, if he were lucky enough to run into the
suspect, Thorne had no intention of apprehending him.
More like aiding him. He would keep that little tidbit
of information to himself for the time being, thank you
very much.

They drove for ten miles past the main intersection,
deeper into the remote stretch of highway.

Leopold had never been out this way before, and the
remoteness of it made her feel like she was in a horror
movie. Images of the car breaking down along side the
road, accompanied with a chain saw wielding lunatic
flashed through her brain. She shifted uncomfortably
in the passenger's seat, and placed her hand on her
Glock for some reassurance.

Breaking the silence, her voice cracked as she spoke, "You have a full tank of gas, right?" Leaning over, she took a look at green iridescent glow of the instrument panel for herself.

Keeping his attention placed on the road, "F," he said dully, "means full, not fill, as far as I know."

Detective Leopold eased back in her seat, and stared out the window, keeping her left hand on the butt of her gun. Thorne didn't seem quite as talkative or quite as amiable as he had been earlier this evening, at the bar. He was being so intense. She had never been paired with him before, so maybe, she thought, this was his "work personality." If so, she was grateful that he wasn't her usual partner. She was almost willing to bet that he wasn't like this with Detective Lenny Shane, or else he would probably get his ass beat.

Detective Thorne slowed the vehicle, and pointed out a dark colored mid sized vehicle that appeared to be abandoned at the entrance to Seminole State Park.

Slowing down, he eased the SUV along side the sedan, and saw that there was no one in the car, and no note posted to the windshield. Glancing over at Leopold, he directed her to stay in the car. Keeping the Jeep running, he undid his seatbelt, and hopped out. Placing his hand on the hood of the car, the coolness of the metal felt good to his palm, on this hot and sticky night.

Thorne jumped back into the Jeep, and looked at Leopold with a stern gaze. With a cool and collected tone, he lied right through his less than perfect teeth, "the hood is still warm, so we probably need to go in and check it out."

Leopold wiped her sweaty palms on her jeans, and nodded to agree. "Let's go," she said.

Thorne clicked his right turn signal on, and pulled into the State Park, pulling his vehicle all the way in to the rear of the parking lot, underneath a burnt out lamp.

He and Detective Leopold exited the vehicle, with the faintest click of their doors. Leopold walked around the rear of the vehicle to where Detective Thorne stood motionless.

Leaning over towards Leopold, he whispered, "I think we should split up, and look around," knowing damn well that there was no one around.

Leopold looked at him with a bit of confusion in her eyes. "Shouldn't we stick together?"

Thorne brushed her question off by replying in a demeaning voice, "Leopold, we'll get more ground covered if we split up. We need to canvas this area, and if it's clear, we need to get back on the road. Do you want this guy to get away? Is that what you want?"

Leopold stammered, "well, no.....but"

Thorne cut her off. "Look, Leopold if you're too scared, or don't have what it takes to do the job, then,...." he let that hang in the air for a moment, knowing his last statement would play on her mind.

Leopold didn't agree with Thorne, but the Lieutenant put her with him for a reason. She was fairly new to this, and he was her superior in a manner of speaking. Not in rank, but in seniority. "You're right," she resided. "Sorry, Thorne."

He placed a reassuring hand on her shoulder. "That's a girl."

They walked together, down a cedar planked walking path, that was lined with forestry on both sides. Coming to a clearing at the end of the path, Thorne signaled her by pointing his finger to go one way, while he started moving in the opposite direction. Clicking on their respective flashlights, they moved out.

Thorne walked about fifty paces, killed his beam of light, and circled back around. Leopold was far enough away, and too busy engaging her senses with her immediate surroundings to notice.

Thorne moved quickly back to the parking lot to grab some necessary tools of his alternative trade. Lifting the rear hatch, he reached into his black duffle bag, and first pulled out some blue latex, surgical quality gloves. Snapping them onto each hand, he flexed his fingers to loosen the snug fit. He decided to skip the hair net cover, because he was associated with Leopold. She was riding in his car, so it would be conceivable, and even probable to find his hair and car fibers on her.

Before zipping the duffle back up, Thorne grabbed the half used roll of grey duct tape, a pair of steel toed boots, and a small cylindrical metal tube, which he tucked into his front pant's pocket. Snugly tucking the roll of tape into the back of his pant's waistline, he removed his wingtip shoes and put the boots on, then closed the rear hatch inaudibly.

Using the trees as cover, Thorne crept quietly closer to Leopold. From behind his bark covered shields, he observed her. She held her flashlight in one hand, and had her other hand resting on the butt of her gun. He stood still, now only ten feet away from her. Patiently he watched, and waited for the perfect moment to present itself to him, while his gloved fingers danced over the small cylindrical metal tube in his pants pocket.

Oblivious to the danger she was actually in, Detective Kate Leopold's nerves had stilled. She was calmly observing the area for any signs of movement, or life, with her eyes peering beyond her beam of light, into the infinite expanse of dark wilderness. There was nothing out here. She didn't see a suspect, and she didn't hear a sound. Not a bird, not a lizard, not a squirrel. It was almost eerie. Was the wildlife aware of something she was not? Was there a top predator around, like a bear, or a panther? Maybe a coyote? *Stop it*, she thought. *You are the top predator, Kate. You have a gun.* Her hand tightened it's grip on the butt of her pistol, and she felt reassured.

Shining her light on the ground, a glint of shimmer sparkled, as it refracted the light. Keeping her light trained on it, she walked closer to it, and saw that it was a glittering length of white-gold chain, with an attached rhinestone encrusted butterfly. Not exactly what she was supposed to be looking for, but as long as she was here, what the hell.

Leopold removed her hand from the butt of her gun, stooped over, and outstretched her hand to pick it up. As the chain dangled off the edge of her fingers, Detective Thorne rushed up behind and tackled her, with the force of a lion taking his prey. The impact caused her to loose her grip on the flashlight, and it sailed through the air in a spinning motion, causing a kaleidoscopic strobe light effect.

Leopold's breath expelled from her lungs in a heave, when the heaviness of her assailant landed on top of her, as they hit the grassy floor in a tangent thud.

Having time, not to think, but only to react, Leopold sent her fists flying, as they rolled around viciously. Throwing a right hook, she felt the sting of flesh being ripped from her knuckles, as they grazed her assailant's teeth. She was struggling to get up off the ground, to disengage from the hand to hand combat, but he was just too big, and too strong.

"Thorne," she screamed frantically, as the weight of the man crushed her. Her assailant had her lying flat on her back. He sat atop her chest, with his legs straddling her sides. Holding her tightly by the wrists, he had her arms outstretched, and pinned firmly to the sides of her head.

"Thorne," she screamed again, more desperately.

Leaning down, she felt his hot breath, as he whispered in her ear, "Yes, Kate, I'm here." He took a deep breath to take in her scent.

Leopold's gamut of emotions fluctuated between relief that it was Thorne, and anger....that it was

Thorne. *What the fuck was he thinking? Whatever it was, this was NOT funny, and she WOULD be reporting him for this.*

"Thorne?" With her anger rising above her feeling of relief, she said, "get the fuck off of me," as she tried to buck him off.

Thorne thought her spunk was cute. He didn't release her, but shifted his grasp of her wrists to one of his hands. He normally didn't play with his victims, but he was nearly bursting out of his jeans. The more they fought, the more turned on he always became. It was when they cried, begged, gave up, and/or pleaded for their lives, that ruined the moment for him. If the moment was ruined, there was no reason to keep them around, because that was just simply boring. This turned out to be the case more often than not.

"Now, why would I do that," he said, taking his free hand and running it down her olive skinned cheek, in between her perky breasts, over her tight stomach, and down her hip towards her gun holster. Removing her gun, he set it back behind him, well out of her reach.

Leopold did not flinch a muscle at the feel of his touch, even though it made her want to vomit. She showed no sign of weakness, and maintained eye contact with his ice blue glare. She could feel her heart racing in her chest, as her breathing quickened. "What the hell are you doing,? Why are you doing this, Thorne," she asked in a frightened tone.

"I'm sorry, Kate," he said slyly. "The "why" is not important, at least not for you to know. What you do need to realize is that you have no chance against me. I'm bigger, I'm stronger, I have your gun, we're in the middle of no where, and you left your cell phone lying on the dash of the car, which I conveniently removed the battery from," he gloated. "There is no use in screaming. No one will hear you. I'm going to let you up, and you're going to do as I say. If you run, I will catch you, even if it's with a bullet. Do you understand?"

Leopold's eyes grew wide, as she realized that this was no joke. She slowly nodded in affirmation, as she suddenly knew that she was about to confirm first-hand, the unknown reason to all of the tension between Thorne and the rest of the team.

Detective Thorne reached behind himself, and grabbed her gun, before letting go of her wrists. With her Glock firmly in his grasp, he released her and quickly stood.

"Stand up, and turn around," he commanded, while waving her own gun at her.

Leopold did as she was told, nice and slow. She kept her hands up, to show him she was not going to try any funny business, and was in full cooperation.

Detective Thorne directed her to walk in the direction of a covered picnic area shelter.

Upon reaching the shelter, he forcefully grabbed a fistful of her shoulder length brown hair on the back of her head, and marched her towards one of the cream-colored plastic picnic tables. Thorne's stride was much larger than Leopold's, causing her tennis shoes to scutter across the ground. Without thinking, her natural reaction to being manhandled was to give Thorne an elbow to the gut. Her heart sank, when it did not faze him or slow his stride. All it did was make him grip her hair even tighter and more forcefully.

"All right," she exclaimed. "I'm going, see? I don't know what your angle here is," she continued, "but, you're out of your fucking mind if you think that you will get away with any of this! Lenny, …I mean, Detective Shane will have your head on a fucking stick! And if not him, then Layne or one of the others!"

Thorne growled, "shut up, bitch! Do not say his fucking name!"

Leopold wrinkled her brow in confusion, as she wondered what the hell that was all about, but she wasn't in the position to worry herself about it at the moment. Her mind was already too busy spinning in a million different directions.

They reached one of the tables at the back of the shelter. There was a dim light streaming in to that corner, from one of the lamps outside the shelter. Nudging her against the table, he took several steps back.

Taking his phone out of his back pocket, he said, "smile for the camera," as he snapped several photos of her, and then tucked his phone back away.

Leopold eyes were no longer adjusted to the dark, thanks to the black sun spots dancing around in them from the flash of the camera. "Take your clothes off. Slowly." he ordered, while waving her gun around.

"Thorne, think about what you're doing. I won't tell anyone what has happened so far," Leopold pleaded.

Thorne sighed loud and audibly in exasperation. It was always the same ass thing. "Listen, honey, I know exactly what I'm about to do, and I've thought about it for a very long time. Just shut your mouth, and do as your told, or I'll tape it shut for you."

Diverting her emerald green eyes towards the floor, Leopold tried to stable her trembling hands, as she reached for the buttons on her blouse. Her fumbling fingers didn't seem to want to work. The harder she tried, the more she shook, at the realization that she was about to be raped.

Thorne grew impatient, and stepped into her space with one large stride. He had no intention of sexually assaulting her, even though his body's response to the stimuli would enable him to. Removing her clothes would make for a cleaner kill. Less chance of evidence being transferred onto the victim. He enjoyed her growing terror, so he would just let her mind continue to create its own hell. It was a sick game, within another sick game. Maybe he would indulge. A little. Rolling his eyes, he said in a bored and blasé tone, "you're taking too long, Kate." Using his long and nimble fingers, he undid all of the buttons on her oxford style shirt with lightning speed.

Leopold leaned backward, and her breath grew ragged, as Thorne's hands opened her shirt completely, and ran over her bare skin. "This is nice," he said while slipping his finger under the strap of her lilac colored lace strewn bra. Victoria's secrets were not going to be secrets for much longer. "I bet Layne would have liked to see you in it." Moving his hands to the front center clasp, he popped it open, and moved both full B sized cups to the side, exposing her soft pink nipples.

Sounding disappointed, he said, "I see you're not as excited as I am." He rubbed his crotch. "I'll have to fix that." Stepping into her, Leopold leaned away from him, as he cupped both of her breasts, and ran his thumbs over her nipples. It did not excite her sexually in the slightest, but she had no control over her body's natural reaction to stimuli. She turned her head to the side, and closed her eyes. Her nipples grew hard, and protruded erect with his touch, which elicited a smile to spread across his face. "Now that's more like it, Kate." His mouth watered to take in her bosom, but he would not. No matter how he would try to explain it, there was no explanation for having his saliva on the victim's breast. Moving one hand down to the buttons of her jeans, he grabbed her face with his other, and cranked her head to face him. "Look at me," he commanded. Leopold felt a lump forming in her throat, and her eyes starting to well up, but she suppressed it. She was not about to give him the satisfaction of seeing the reaction he was seeking from her.

Leopold closed her eyes, and kept telling herself to just picture someone else. Picture Layne, picture Layne, she kept repeating inside her head. It seemed to help somewhat, but she was not that open minded. No matter what she kept telling herself, she knew who it was…and she knew who it wasn't. She came to conclude that she could always just pretend that she

was getting a bad Gyno checkup. The one good thing
was that he was wearing gloves. At least he wasn't
actually touching her flesh with his.

With Leopold now glaring at him with an evil hatred
in her eyes, Thorne moved down to the button of her
jeans. He unsnapped the button fly's, and tugged the
jeans down over her hips. Running his palms over the
hourglass figure of her waist, he slipped them
underneath her matching panties, running his hands
over her nicely rounded buttocks, and yanked them
down to her mid thighs. Glancing down at her, his
heart sped with anticipation, and his shaft stirred. As
he lightly brushed her clean shaven skin with his
gloved fingertips, her face contorted in revulsion. This
really made him ache for release.

Thorne took a few steps back, and Leopold sighed a
breath of relief, because she thought that this
nightmare was all over. Maybe he was just some
pervert getting a cheap thrill at her expense, and it
would be her word against his, and nothing more.
Stopping mid reach to redress herself, Leopold's gut
wrenched in despair when Thorne spoke.

"Turn around, and pull your pants, and your panties
off," Thorne ordered.

Turning around slowly, with her back to him, she
stripped to be completely naked. Standing there, she
crossed her arms across her chest, and covered her bare
breasts.

While Leopold was getting undressed, Thorne
removed the roll of duct tape from the back of his
waistline. Grabbing Leopold's hands from behind, he
pried them from her breasts, and cranked them behind
her. A small whimper escaped Leopold's lips. Thorne
brushed her hair to the side, and grabbed her by the
chin, firmly, but not forcefully. "Shhhh. You're gonna
help me make it all better, Kate. Don't you want to
help me make it all better, Kate?" Leopold couldn't
speak through her quivering lips, as Thorne bound

her wrists with the tape.

"Sit down," he ordered her, pointing at the seat of the picnic table. Leopold was utterly confused, but also relieved. Sitting hunched over, with her breasts covered from Thorne's line of sight by the table top, she furiously dug at the tape trying to get her hands unbound. She watched in confusion as Thorne picked up her tennis shoe, and removed something from his pocket. He inserted whatever it was into the groove of her shoe tread, then pounded the sole of the shoe on the table, forcing whatever he took out of his pocket, to become lodged within the treads of her shoe. With her police instincts kicking into high gear, she thought that it might be a tracking device?

Leopold was perspiring tremendously, and not just because of the current dire situation she found herself in. It was an exceptionally sweltering July. Lows in the eighties, even when the sun went down. Under normal circumstances, she would curse her antiperspirant for not working effectively. Tonight, the slick moisture permeating her skin helped her to slide her hands out of the tape. Balling it in her fist, she threw it behind Thorne, over his head. He fell for the distraction, and looked behind him. Without any hesitation, Leopold grabbed her shirt and her shoes off the table, and took off like a bat out of hell.

With her bare feet pounding over the dry grass, her arms pumped like two well oiled machines. She ran for the cover of darkness, amidst the trees and shrubbery. If she could just loose him and hide until daybreak, she might have a chance. Glancing quickly behind her, she saw that Thorne was not too far behind. Giving it all she had, she darted into the tree line, and weaved in and around the native fauna. She did not stop at the first good cover she came across, because she felt that would be too obvious. It would be the first place he would look. Her lungs were burning, and her feet were now stinging from slight abrasions caused by her

naked pedicured feet racing over the unkempt
ground.. She didn't want to stop running, but the sharp
pain in the side of her abdomen, demanded she did.
Stopping briefly to catch her breath, she took short,
fast breaths through her nose. She slipped her tennis
shoes on, and crudely tied them before taking off
again.

With her feet protected, she could move much more
quickly. She was able to slip her shirt back on and
button it up, although it was like trying to get dressed
while doing jumping jacks. Her pupils were fully
dilated, as she scanned the area ahead for some cover.
She would have to scan, and make a split second
decision as to whether to hide or continue running.
There was no time for indecisiveness.

About thirty feet ahead, she saw a nice thick cluster
of bushes. She could nuzzle herself deep within it's
bowels, and it would offer ample cover. Aiming
straight for it, Leopold glanced again over her
shoulder. She did not see Thorne, so she went for it.

Her heart was hammering in her chest, and she could
barely swallow with the dryness of her throat. Her legs
were quivering beneath her, but she kept on pushing.
She was closing in, only fifteen more feet to go, and
she could give herself a much needed rest. Having a
finish line burst of energy, she started running as fast
as she could, towards the thick expanse of bushes.
Once again, glancing over her shoulder, as her feet
were moving full speed, she did not see Thorne behind
her.

As Leopold turned her head back around to look
where she was going, she didn't have time to stop;
although, her heart nearly did, as her eyes focused on
what lie ahead. Thorne stepped out of nowhere, and
she was on a one way collision course, right into him.
Thorne spread his arms wide, in a welcoming embrace.
"Ahh. There you are," he said in a victorious manner.
Leopold tried to divert, but she ran straight into him.

Thorne absorbed the wave of energy from her speed,
and redirected it by grabbing her by the shoulders, and
forcefully throwing her to the ground, like a little rag
doll. A wave of pain emanated from Leopold's right
side, as it smacked the dry unforgiving ground.

Thorne wasted no time, by allowing her to get up.
Time was wasting, and this little bitch needed to be
taken care of. Leopold cried out in pain, as Thorne
started kicking her forcefully, about the torso and face.
Feeling helpless, Leopold curled herself into a tight
ball, and tried to cover her face with her forearms. It
was a futile effort against Thorne's savage assault.

As her body was severely ravaged, her breaths
became harder and harder to take. They came in short,
hard, sucks. She equated it to the same feeling you get
when you swallow water down your windpipe. It was
getting harder to breathe, and it was getting harder to
see through her swollen eyes. She could taste the
distinct metallic taste of blood in her mouth. Leopold
realized that she had gone into shock, when she could
no longer feel the intense pain that accompanied
Thorne's blows. She knew that her end was near, and
silently made her peace with her maker, before she
took her last shallow and painful breath.

Thorne stopped as abruptly as he started. Sensing his
job here was finished, he knelt down beside the now,
unrecognizably bruised and swollen Kate Leopold.
Panting, he took his gloved middle and forefinger, and
placed them on her neck, directly on her carotid. Just
as he suspected, her blood ceased to flow, and was as
still as a frozen pond. He felt no pulsating veins
beneath her olive skin.

Thorne retrieved the rest of her clothing from the
base of a nearby tree. He fully redressed her, minus her
gun and holster, then pulled out his cell phone again.

Flashes of light lit up the darkness. "Oh yeah. Work
that camera, baby," he said, as he snapped shots of his
gruesome handiwork.

Taking her gun, he fired two random shots. He dumped it, her holster, and her phone battery into a trash bin on the way back to his vehicle.

Opening up the Jeep's rear cargo hatch, he calmly removed the boots, the gloves, and the tape. He neatly placed them back into his duffle bag, and stowed it under the cargo area, next to the spare tire.

Moving into the restroom, Thorne studied himself in the mirror, and was pleased with what he saw. The only wound he had, was a small split on the inside of his bottom lip, but it was not visible. Turning on the tap, he ran his hands beneath the lukewarm water, and splashed his face with it. He soaped and scrubbed his hands well, with the hotel quality hand soap, before drying them with a hot blast of electric air.

Glancing at his Timex, he saw that this little incident had taken longer than he had originally anticipated. Knowing that Leopold would eventually be identified, and that would likely lead to his questioning, didn't matter to him. By the time that happened, his plan would be in full swing. It was nearly time for phase two of the plan. He would leave her here for a Park Ranger, or an unsuspecting hiker to find and call in. Right now, he had places to go, things to do, and someone else to abduct.

# 4. ON THE RUN

CONSIDERING the Atlantic was to his East, and if he were to head South towards the Florida Keys, he would run out of land, Robert Verde knew that the most heavily patrolled areas would be to the West and to the North. The "po-po," or so his nickname was for the police, would most likely be expecting him to head either North or West, to hit an interstate in order to flee out of the state.

So much for what they thought, because he would do just the opposite of what he knew they expected him to do. Just not quite yet. He needed to find food and shelter, and just lay low for awhile, and let the urgent buzz fizzle out.

Verde blended into his environment, within the tourist filled metropolis streets. He knew it was much

easier to elude police by being in a big city, than
fleeing into some small podunk town.

Keeping his red brimmed hat pulled low, Robert
Verde strolled leisurely down the busy streets.
Walking past all of the designer shops and upscale
restaurants, he continued walking until he came upon a
more average area of town. Verde saw the familiar and
immediately recognizable red and yellow glowing
franchise sign of a McDonald's. He walked back
towards the fast food chain's dumpster, took a seat
under the shadow of a palm tree, and waited. He hoped
that someone would come out soon, because his
stomach was rumbling, and the smell permeating the
air, was about to make him start salivating. Literally.

Within the hour, a skinny pimply faced teenage boy,
brought out a goldmine concealed in black plastic, and
whipped it into the large green dumpster. Verde
watched and waited until he walked back through the
employee only back door, before making a move.
Immediately digging out the just placed large black
plastic bag, Verde slung it over his shoulder, and took
off in a light jog, into an adjacent industrial
warehouse's rear parking lot. He could feel the left
over warmth from the fast food chain's heating lamps
emanating through the plastic, warming his back.
Smelling of fried oil, and grilled meat, he didn't even
have to open the bag to know that he had hit pay dirt.

Finding a nice curb stop to dine on, Verde parked his
rump on the paved lot and furiously ripped the bag
open. The smell of warm, greasy goodness lingered up
into his nostrils. Rustling through the smorgasbord, he
found loads of still wrapped cheeseburgers, big macs,
chicken nuggets, and various other menu items. He
knew from being on the run once before, that fast food
chains often threw out perfectly good food, because it
had been sitting under the heat lamps too long to fit
their corporate freshness standards.

As he sat there savoring his late moonlit dinner for

one, he started scoping out his immediate surrounding area. Looking at the mustard-yellow colored metal corrugated building directly in front of him, he counted ten large bays. Each one had a roll up type garage door, along with a regular door. He saw no alarm monitoring systems, or building video surveillance in place. This would be a perfect spot to lie in wait, with food and if needed, a restroom right next door.

Verde approached the building, and started to walk it's length. Cautiously he checked each door, and each bay latch to see if it was unlocked. Framing his vision with his hands, he placed his face against the glass to peek inside the windows, before doing so.

Verde was starting to get discouraged, until he came upon the seventh door. When he jiggled the door handle, the door popped open. Slowly opening it, he cautiously poked his head in to take a look inside. The place was an interior decorator's dream. It was filled with couches, chairs, loveseats, armoires, beds, mirrors, night stands, desks, and all other sorts of home furnishings. With no one around, Verde walked in and closed the door, locking it behind him. Grabbing the door handle, he twisted and shook it, to make sure the lock wasn't defective. Satisfied he would be safe and sound, he walked directly to the right rear of the space, finding a small, well decorated office, and flipped on the light. He settled himself behind the executive style cherry wood desk, into the oversized dark leather computer chair. Looking around the top of the desk, he saw a business card holder that held black cards with silver metallic lettering in a fancy script that said: "Final Touches Home Staging." *That would explain all the furniture*, Verde thought. Rifling through the desk drawers, he didn't find anything except standard office supplies, until he looked in the largest bottom drawer. Pulling out a bank deposit bag, he unzipped it to reveal a petty cash stash of five hundred dollars. Pulling the loot out of the bag, he fanned the soft paper through his fingers, smelled it, and gave it a kiss before tucking the wad into his pocket. "Today must be my lucky day."

With his belly full, and a place to rest, Verde wanted to settle in for the night. His curiosity got the better of him, and he just had to check the net before drifting off. Reaching over to the computer's keyboard, Verde Googled the local Miami area's top stories. Sure enough, there he was, right at the top, which included a rough sketch of his face. His eyes scanned the headline: "Serial Murderer Escapes Miami Dade Correctional Facility." The article went on to detail the discovery of his absence by the staff at the prison, a warning to the public regarding how dangerous he was, and the area wide manhunt that had been launched to apprehend him.

Verde leaned back in the soft leather chair, and clucked his dry mouth. Walking over to the mini fridge in the office, he scanned his thirst quenching options, and settled on pouring himself a nice glass of pinot noir. Raising his white styrofoam cup, he made a toast to himself for being victorious. Settling back behind the desk, he relished the taste of the fine wine, as he sipped on it. He leisurely continued searching the net for various things, one of which included nearby marinas.

Some time later, Verde glanced at the lower right corner of the computer screen, and saw that it was two o'clock in the morning. He had been surfing the internet for nearly an hour. He had obtained enough information to plan his next move, so he could rest easy now.

Clearing the history on the computer screen, and wiping his prints off of the desk and computer, Verde got up from behind the desk, and walked out into the warehouse area. He settled himself upon a black Italian leather sectional, that did not face the window of the shop. Fluffing up the cream colored throw pillows that were randomly placed on the sofa, he made himself comfortable and drifted off, dreaming of his new future.

# 5. ABDUCTION

BOBBY Thorne sat and waited patiently, drumming his fingers on the steering wheel. The black Lincoln Continental he was driving was…borrowed, while his Jeep Grand Cherokee took up residency in the Lincoln's usual garage spot. Ms. Hinkle was his snowbird neighbor, that was only in Naples for three months out of the year. She paid him to keep an eye on her house, and to start her Lincoln periodically when she was out of town from April through December. It prevented the engine from seizing up, or so he convinced her. Old women were so easy to manipulate. All he had to do was turn on the charm and he could have them eating out of the palm of his hand. For the nine months she was back in New Jersey, the Italian widower with the big black bouffant hair and even bigger mouth, which was always meticulously coated with hot pink lipstick, had no idea that he drove her Lincoln on occasion, to pursue his extracurricular activities. It was perfect for covering his tracks and keeping his secret agendas hidden. He could do without the pine car fresher stinging his nose, though; although, he preferred it over whatever God awful perfume she always doused herself in that smelled like potpourri scented mothballs.

He had been parked two doors down, adjacent to 5252 Palm Drive, in front of a foreclosed house. There were several foreclosures on the street, but this one offered a perfect view point for his current interest. He rolled in to his destination at 6:00 am, still under a blanket of night, in the black car with the dark tinted windows, in his black clothing and blue latex gloves. This had been his routine on Monday through Friday, for the last two weeks, except earlier this evening, his normal routine of wake up at 4:00 am, hit the gym, grab something fast and easy for breakfast, head to Palm Drive, survey the house, wait for the bastard to leave, go to work, go home, repeat, had been interrupted. An serendipitous opportunity had presented itself, and he just couldn't resist.

Seeing an amber glow emerge from the large bay window, his thin lips parted and curled upwards to reveal a crooked smile filled with evil delight. Glancing at his Timex, it read 6:15.

"Right on cue," he whispered to no one.

He was like a cat that had spotted it's prey. His eyes were locked onto the target, his body went rigid, and the hunted had no idea he was about to strike.

Reaching over to the passenger seat, his hand glided over the coolness of the light grey leather. Finding the binoculars, he set them on his wide, twice previously broken nose. Abusive foster homes had left him with not only physical reminders of his youth, but emotional scars that still festered. He was no one's victim. Not anymore.

The sight of the petite blonde made him flush. A wave of heat, that was not from the humid air outside blasted his body. Setting the binoculars back on the seat, he switched the key to auxiliary mode and the arctic blast chilled his balmy skin. Sticking his face close to the vents, he closed his eyes briefly. His skull buzzed hair stood unwavering in the artificial breeze. The droplets on his forehead dissipated, and he switched the ignition back to the off position.

Turning his attention back over to the large bay window, his eyes narrowed in despise.

The blonde woman, Tessa, and her husband, Detective Lenny Shane, were doing their usual smoochy-goodbye routine. His once drumming fingers gripped the steering wheel so tightly that his fingers ached. His entire body pulsed with tremors, like the Earth quaking. He chuckled quietly to himself in a foreboding tone.

He hated that bastard for what he did, and he was going to pay. An eye for an eye. Tessa wasn't really the object of his despise…she was just a necessary pawn in his game, just like Kate Leopold. Collateral damage. He harbored no feelings of guilt or empathy for anyone or anything. His mind was a one way track that led straight to revenge. He was going to get it, and he wasn't letting anyone get in the way, and he didn't care who got hurt in the process. He had worked very hard to get to this point. Years. As the plan required, he assumed a new life, complete with a new identity. He took that from a vagrant, whose body was never found. Now that the payoff was so close, anticipation rose over him. Today was the day that his plan would finally be set into motion.

The buzzing street lamps on Palm Drive silenced as the life flickered out of them. The squealing sound of the garage door opening was the intro to his masterpiece. It sounded like nails over a chalk board.

Most people cringed at the sound, but he delighted in it.

Detective Lenny Shane roared out of his garage on his custom v-twin in his usual couture, with his shoulder length grey hair blowing in the breeze, and his Harley sunglasses covering his dark chocolate eyes. He was dressed in his typical cowboy boots, Wranglers, white oxford with a bolo, and a vest. The man in the Lincoln rolled his eyes at his predictable routine. 7:00 am on the dot. So. Fucking. Dull. He was hoping that this might be somewhat of a challenge. Some fun.

As Detective Lenny Shane grew smaller in the distance, Bobby Thorne stepped out of the Lincoln, onto Palm Drive, and closed the driver's side door with the faintest click. He threw his back pack of goodies over one shoulder.

Leaning against the car, watching Lenny until he completely disappeared, he said in a snarky tone, "I hope you like the present I left you. Detective. Shane."

He strode quickly across the Palm lined street to the rear of the house. Reaching into his back pack, he pulled out a black ski mask and slid it over his buzzed dome. Peering into a side window, he saw Tessa finish the last of the breakfast dishes. She had an iPod clipped to her hip and was dancing around like a fool. She dried her hands on a dish towel that was hanging from the oven handle, then wiped the remaining wetness off on her grey velvet sweats. He watched her saunter down the hallway, into the last room on the left. Her Sketchers were doing a squeaking song of their own on the ceramic tile, but he was sure she couldn't hear the sneaker music over the Aerosmith blaring through her Dr. Dre Beats headphones.

The long sliders slid open without a sound. Peering down the hallway, he closed them slowly, as if he were diffusing a bomb. The lock clicked into place. His 185lb lanky body floated across the floor as if it were made of air. He knew what room Tessa had gone into, because this was not the first time he had been in the house.

He tip-toed down the hallway, stopping briefly to admire the woman's wildlife photographs that were lined up like soldiers on the beige wall. He particularly liked the one of the alligators. Vicious and powerful predators, they were. Lurking just beneath a murky surface waiting for their unsuspecting prey. Reminded him a bit of himself. He wondered briefly how long it would take them to notice if he just took it home with him, but decided it was a bad idea.

He squatted down behind the last door on the left. Red light from the photography dark room peaked through the door frame. He flung the back pack off of his right shoulder and carefully placed it just outside the door. Opening the pack, he reached in and grabbed a white terry cloth towel, and a bottle of his homemade chloroform. It was so easy to make. A couple of ingredients from your local drugstore, and wahlah. He soaked the cloth with the dreamtime liquid, replaced the cap, and set the brown glass bottle back into the pack, with a gentle carefulness.

Thorne placed his unwavering latex bound hand firmly on the brass door handle. He was as calm as the eye of a hurricane. A sneak attack was not necessary, but he took great delight in not only assailing his victims physically, but also psychologically. The horror that exuded from their wide eyes and screaming mouths was orgasmic to his senses. The handle rotated with slow precision. Placing his left palm on the door, he pulled it open as gently as a Mother cradles her child. The door did not make a sound. Fortunately, it wasn't in desperate need of some WD-40, like the garage door. The sight of Tessa being consumed in the red light made him fantasize of bathing her in the crimson liquid that pulsed through her veins. Unlike most serial killers, he wasn't picky about how he killed his victims. Variety, after all was the spice of life, or so they said. Changing it up kept it fresh and exciting. His breath quickened as his four chambered heart beat ferociously in his chest. His excitement radiated out from his core.

Tessa's brow furrowed with annoyance and anger as she realized some dumb ass just ruined her remaining undeveloped photos, as her thick red light, became diluted with a rush of clean white light. Thinking it was probably her annoyingly nosy neighbor, Mr. Perkins, who seemed to think it was okay to come in and out of the neighborhood's houses without knocking, she said "What the fuck, don't you know you can't-------- " as she wheeled around, with her arms up similar to that I don't know gesture.

Her steam was quickly released as she realized that it was not Mr. Perkins.

Startled, she let out a blood curling scream upon seeing a large masked man advancing quickly towards her. Even though the shrill sound pierced his eardrums, he welcomed it. The veins in her neck protruded through her ivory skin from the force of air bellowing through her wind pipe. She put her hands up in a defensive gesture, but he was as quick as a cobra. The impact slammed her against the stationary steel work table. Her sciatic nerve released a river of pain that flowed down her buttocks and legs. He had her pinned onto the table, with his forearm across her chest. Her small 120lb. frame was bearing all of his crushing weight. The coolness of the steel sent shivers down her spine. Her arms flailed and sent her Nikon and film rolls crashing to the floor. He engulfed her face with the drenched white cloth, pressing it firmly to conceal all of her airways. Her cries were now muffled as the poison was inhaled. In a natural reaction to escape the foul stench, she cocked her head to the side. The toxic fumes raped her throat, and her neck muscles strained from the stretch. Inside her ears, a high frequency buzz blocked out all other sound. The man's face became indistinct and blurred as the poison invaded her nervous system.

Like the flip of a switch, her mind suddenly went into survival mode, as her lungs begged for clean oxygen. Her legs were running a race, but her body was going nowhere, as they flailed in the air. Tessa desperately clawed at her assailant's wrists and arms, because she could not reach his face. She would have went for his eyes if she could. He felt the hot slices of her French manicured daggers ripping his skin as it gathered under her nails. Feeling a warm flow trickle down his arm, he glanced over to see how badly the bitch had broken his skin. Tessa felt the weight on her chest ease ever so slightly, and in a split decision used all of her strength to bring her right knee up into his jewels. Hard.

She could see the man's eyes grow wide in shock, through the eye holes of his masked face, as he completely released her to cup his throbbing manhood.

Doubling over in pain, a roaring "fucking whore!" escaped his tongue. She felt his hot spit spew onto her face.

As he headed towards the ground, Tessa shoved him and stumbled towards the door. Her head was spinning, and her feet were unsteady. As she rounded the door frame, she glanced back and could see the fuzzy image of him in a fetal position, writhing in pain, and moaning in utter agony.

Tessa's mind was willing her tingling numb feet to move faster, but they would not cooperate. Her mind was clear enough to know that she needed to get to the kitchen to get her cell phone. Help was only three button pushes away. Rounding out the door, she felt her foot get caught on something, and started falling forward. Glancing down, all she could make out was a small lump of darkness. She sailed through the air towards the ceramic tile. She willed her arms to break her fall, but they didn't move fast enough. Her skull hit

the ground with a deafening crack. Everything grew
dark.

Thorne's intense pain finally subsided. He scrambled
to get to his feet as he heard a loud commotion in the
hallway. His only thought was that he needed to get the
hell out of there. Fast. She was probably already out of
the house, or on her cell phone calling 911, or worse,
the man that was her husband and his partner,
Detective Lenny Shane. It wasn't time for that yet.

Briskly moving towards the door, he peered down the
hallway. Glancing down, he saw Tessa sprawled out,
face down. His backpack was tangled around her right
ankle. She was out cold, with a small pool of blood
oozing out from under her head. The corners of his
mouth curled upward, and he clapped sarcastically.

"Bravo. Bravo, Tessa," he said as he approached her.

He kneeled beside her and placed his big palm on her
back. Feeling her rise and fall, he muttered in a
mocking tone, "Ah. Good. I was really hoping you
didn't kill yourself, because I'm not done with you or
your husband yet." As he spoke, he emphasized the
word, really. He drew it out in a long draw, so it
sounded more like reeeeeeeeally.

He untangled his back pack from her limp foot. He
unzipped the pack and removed a roll of duct tape, a
spool of nylon rope, and a hunting knife. The first
piece of tape went across her mouth. He liked it when
she was screaming, but he didn't want anyone else to
hear her. He needed to get her somewhere more
isolated first. Making quick work of it, he cranked her
arms behind her back. Holding her wrists together with
one hand, he used his other to wind the gray sticky
stuff tightly around and around her bare skin. Moving
to her ankles, he bound them in the same way. He
grabbed the nylon rope and used the hunting knife to
cut a six foot length of it. He bent her knees up towards
the ceiling, and used the rope to marry her wrists and
ankles. She was going to have to stay put for awhile,

while he kept up appearances.

Satisfied she was going no where, he strode down the hallway, and into the kitchen. He pocketed her iPhone that was laying on the counter, and went out the side door to the garage. Pushing the garage opener with his spindly fingers, the door started to squeal as the motor turned the crank. Wanting to keep a low profile, he removed his ski mask, and hung it on the shiny doorknob. People might not pay too much attention to a stranger walking across the street, but they would definitely pay attention if he were wearing a ski mask. Ducking his six foot frame under the moving garage door, he strode quickly towards the Lincoln, with his head down.

Reaching inside his black cargo pants pocket, he pulled out the keys and hit the unlock button. A chirp, chirp was the only sound on the deserted street besides his size twelve black wingtips slapping the pavement.

Settled comfortably in the leather bucket, he did a three hundred sixty look around. He didn't see a soul stirring on the residential drive. The engine purred and he pulled forward. He backed into the garage and popped the trunk before turning the car off. He stepped out of the vehicle and watched the garage door close with a final thud.

Tessa was still out of it. In her unconsciousness, she dreamed of floating lazily in a sea of nothingness. Periodic flashes of warm, bright light pierced through her veil of darkness. Serenity settled over her, and she let the river carry her weightless body downstream.

He flung Tessa's limp body over his shoulder with ease. He carried her out to the garage, and placed her inside the trunk of the Lincoln. He brushed the sticky red hair off of her forehead. *Ouch. That's going to hurt,* he thought. He slammed the lid shut with a triumphant look spreading across his face.

Firing up the Lincoln, the clock radio read 7:20. He pulled out of the garage at and eased down Palm Drive,

heading back to Ms. Hinkle's garage. He would leave
Tessa to her nice little nap in the trunk of the Lincoln,
while he took his Jeep to go to work. He sat behind
the wheel, grinning from ear to ear, like a kid in a
candy store.

# 6. OUT TO SEA

VERDE woke from the best sleep he had in twenty years. Sitting up, he raised himself off of the plush leather sectional, just as the sun was starting to rise. He raised both of his arms, in a full body stretch, and smiled because his back didn't hurt, for the first time in twenty years. Sleeping on something that was thicker and more plush than a wafer, must have that effect.

Slipping his shoes on, he shuffled into the bathroom. Locking the door behind him, he undressed down to his boxers, and walked over to the double sink vanity. Turning the water on, he stuck his head into the sink, and let the water cascade over his head and face. Pulling up on the sink stopper, he let the basin fill with warm water and two squirts of ocean breeze scented hand soap, that he pumped out of an ornate looking soap dispenser. He took what his Mama had always referred to as a whore bath, and redressed.

He headed out into the morning, with his red ball cap over his damp hair, and his head low. His stomach rumbled, but he had one stop to make beforehand. Thanks to his internet search of the local area, he knew exactly where he was heading. He had to walk two blocks down.

Browsing around inside the Walgreens, Verde filled his green plastic hand held basket with a bunch of items he needed to help with disguising himself. Things like glasses and hair color. Making his way to the cashier at the front of the store, he also filled the basket with a bunch of shit he probably didn't need. Like smokes, and stuff like chocolate covered donuts.

Once outside, Verde put the shopping bags inside the Florida beach bum beach bag he had just purchased. He slipped on some mirrored aviator style glasses, and lit a smoke. Leisurely strolling back towards the warehouse, Verde snuffed his smoke out in the ashtray provided on top of a trash can, before going into the McDonalds to grab a hot cakes and sausage breakfast, a large coffee, and a large orange juice.

The entire warehouse building was as vacant as a ghost town.. He walked right back into the door at Final Touches Home Staging, that he had left unlocked.

Settling himself behind the desk in the office, Verde Googled a little more info in between choking down his breakfast. He swallowed his last bite and grabbed a pen and a piece of paper, before picking up the phone to dial.

Cradling the phone between his ear and shoulder, Verde spoke: "Hey, it's me… Yeah, I'm okay…I'm happy too…Okay…That's what I thought too…Uh-huh….I'm headed to the marina this morning…Where am I going, what's your address?…Got it. See you soon…I will…Bye."

Verde hung the phone up, and stuffed the information into his jeans pocket.

He slurped down the last of his orange juice, and walked back to the bathroom, with his beach bag in tow. Pulling out a small grey box, he read the instructions explicitly. He mixed the two bottles of liquid into the applicator bottle. A foul smell of ammonia filled the air. Verde snapped on the oversized plastic gloves, and squeezed the gelatin like substance onto his hair. He covered it with a plastic cap, and waited.

Thirty minutes later, Verde emerged from the restroom, looking and feeling like a new man. His hair under his red baseball cap, was now a natural looking chestnut brown. He carried the jeans and crocks in his beach bag, because he was sporting a new pair of flip flops and light blue swimming trunks printed with the outlines of different types of fish.

Looking and feeling like he was on vacation…well, duh, he was on a vacation… of sorts, he cleaned and erased all traces of him ever being there, and walked out into the sweltering Miami summer heat.

#

Verde pulled a wad out of the beach bag, and handed the cab driver twenty bucks.

"Keep the change," Verde said, as he exited the canary yellow taxi.

"Gracias. Muchas gracias," beamed the over zealous, middle-aged Latino driver.

Verde slowly approached the tick tack toe board-ish expanse of dock. His eyes surveyed the area for movement of any kind. He could always walk the dock, and look for a craft complete with keys, but that may look too suspicious if someone saw him obviously scoping the joint out. The last thing he needed was for the cops to be called.

The easiest and least attention drawing method, was to become someone's uninvited guest.

Verde's stomach swarmed with butterflies, as his long suppressed and depraved monster started to awaken. He stood there, with his eyes glazed over the endless cobalt blue. That was one of the many beautiful things about the sea. Not only was she beautiful to look at, but she could be a willing and able accomplice.

From his vantage point at the beginning of the dock, he only saw three people. Just down from where he stood, there was a golden skinned, shirtless middle aged man, with overgrown bleach blonde hair, whose chest and arm muscles bulged as he was scooping ice from the ice chest, and packing it into his two red rolling coolers. Too big. Too much work to take him down, and he wasn't into running the risk of getting taken down himself. Further down and out, there was a yuppyish bean pole twenty something, on a sail boat. Verde supposed his name was Winston. Or Thornton the III, or some other proper like sissy shit name like that, who wouldn't of lasted two seconds where he just came from. Easy target. Shitty boat. Too slow.

Behind his aviator mirrored sunglasses, Verde's eyes narrowed in on a buxom beauty in a provocative little sundress. With her golden glowing skin and platinum blonde hair, she looked like either a stripper, or a Hawaiian Tropic girl. He was too far away to tell. He felt himself grow hard at the thought of any woman. He had been in prison for such a long time, that he would take either one.

He strode with purpose towards the medium sized craft. It had a below deck cabin, in which he could stow away until they got out to sea. *Perfect.*

#

By the time Verde reached the craft, the woman was
entirely too busy standing at the helm, having a heated
bitch fest on her cell phone. She didn't hear or see him
board the boat.

He moved quickly below decks, hiding inside the
bathroom. Verde rolled his eyes, and took an impatient
seat on the porcelain throne to listen to the heated
banter.

"You know what, bitch? You two can have each
other. You're a slut, and he's a piece of shit! No!
We're not friends. We *were* friends, until you and MY
boyfriend decided to fuck each other. Slut. You know
what, I gotta go, but you and Brad have a nice life. Oh,
and Mandy? Both of you lose my number, and don't
look me up when he cheats on you too!"

Verde heard a clamoring noise, that he supposed was
her cell phone being hurdled across the boat, followed
by, "Asshole!" The drama, oh the drama. The motor
fired up, and they started to move.

Verde walked out of the bathroom, and stretched out
on the soft bed. As long as the boat was moving, she
would be at the helm, and would be none the wiser of
her guest.

Thirty minutes into the rocking ride, they slowed, and
the engine was cut. He bounded off the bed, and took
refuge back on his porcelain throne, leaving the door
cracked enough that he had a view of the entire cabin
area.

Thorne eyed Blondie as she descended down the
short flight of stairs, into the interior cabin. Walking
over to the bureau, she was still mumble bitching to
herself. Grasping the elastic top of the strapless baby
blue number, she yanked it off.

Thorne's manhood immediately stirred at the sight of
her naked body, and grew even harder when watching
her spray and rub the coconut scented tanning oil all

over herself. She sprayed her legs, and bent over to rub the oil in, with her back to where Verde was perched. He got an eyeful of her tanned heart shaped ass and pink slit.

He quickly ditched his swimming trunks onto the floor, and swung the door open. Blondie pivoted around completely startled. And gloriously naked. Verde quickly closed the gap between the two of them, as Blondie started to scream. Not knowing what else to do, she used the only thing she had immediate access to, and gave his face a good dose of Coppertone.

Verde swatted the can out of her hand. It clamored onto the floor, and rolled across the cabin towards the opposite wall. Clamping his other hand over her cosmetically enhanced lips, he got her under control.

Spinning her around, and putting her in a choke hold, he walked her towards the bed. In a calm voice, he said, "if you scream, I'm going to hurt you." Which, was a complete and total lie. He was going to hurt her either way.

He had never assaulted a woman in this fashion before, but it had been what? Almost twenty years since he was with a woman. Verde had his way with her. When he was completely exhausted, and unable to perform, he lit a smoke, and took a seat on an armchair, where he could still see Blondie lying on the bed in her quivering fetal position, which was as, if not more enjoyable to him as the sex.

# 7. LET THE GAMES BEGIN

AS DETECTIVE Lenny Shane cruised down US 41, he reached into the inside left breast pocket of his tan suede vest. Feeling the two rigid tickets to paradise he had purchased at AAA made him anxious. It wasn't just a nine night Mexican Riviera trip he was giving Tessa. She had been wanting him to retire his badge so they could travel and spend more time together. He struggled with it, because being a Detective was his identity. It was all he knew. But, there wasn't anything he wouldn't do for her, so he was anxious to see the ecstatic look it would put on her face.

He just wanted to get through this Friday as quickly as possible, and take his honey to that fancy steak house, Ruth's Chris to celebrate their life of thirty wonderful years together. Well, thirty wonderful years

for him...her, not so much the whole time. It was also
a good start to their next chapter. He had made
reservations for 7:00 pm, two weeks ago. Nothing was
going to ruin this day.

Lenny pulled his candy apple red custom motorcycle
into the parking lot at the Naples Police Department.
He dismounted his iron horse, and used his sleeve to
polish a print off of the gas tank. He had waited a long
time to get her, and he was damn glad that Tessa
wanted that kitchen remodel more than she didn't want
him getting a motorcycle. It was an even trade. She got
her kitchen, he got his bike.

Walking into the precinct, his Lieutenant, Sara
Witten, a fire cracker of a redhead, motioned him into
her office. She looked svelte as usual in her navy blue
pantsuit, with her hair piled loosely on top of her head,
as it always was. She handed him a cup of coffee
exactly the way he liked it. Black. Just black, no
cream, no sugar. "Shane," she said in a grim voice, "I
know we all had a long night last night, but after you
drink this, I need you to hop back on that motorcycle
of yours and head over to the Seminole State Park. I
received a call about five minutes ago from dispatch.
Detectives Wilshire and Layne are already on their
way there."

She sighed as she leaned with the fingers of both
hands splayed on top of her file strewn mahogany
desk, and shook her head in discontent. "A body has
been discovered. Young female. Beaten so badly, she's
unidentifiable. A couple of uniforms are already on the
scene. I gave them strict instructions to tape it off, and
not to touch anything. They are waiting for some of my
guys to get there. Forensics will be right behind you."
She stood erect and placed her hands on her hips.

Lenny swallowed a long slow sip of his black java.
Raising his mug as if making a toast he said, "Just
another day at the office. I'm on it Lieutenant." He
reached over and put his free hand on her shoulder and

gave it a light squeeze to console her. "Don't worry. We'll get the son of a bitch. I promise."

She nodded in appreciation of his gesture, and gave him a faint smile. "I never doubt your skills, Detective Shane. Or your fabulous use of resources. Your methods might sometimes be outside the box, but you always get the job done."

Completely changing the mood, she peered around Lenny through the wall of windows in her office that looked out over her team, and said, "And where the hell are Leopold and Thorne?"

Lenny glanced back towards the sea of metal desks. "Sorry, Lieutenant. Haven't seen them or heard from them."

"Well," she sighed. "If you see or talk to either one, tell them to get their asses over there. Pronto."

He nodded once, and just as cool as a cucumber said, "We'll do."

Lenny sucked down the rest of his freshly brewed java. Exiting the station, he hopped back on his bike, and headed towards Seminole State Park, on the outskirts of town. During the thirty minute ride, his mind drifted.

Thorne was a good partner…when he decided to show up on time. Lenny was on the fence about letting him sleep in the bed he was making for himself. He was no rat, but man he was getting tired of covering for the dude. Sara wasn't just his Lieutenant. She was a long time colleague as well as a friend, and he didn't like lying to her to cover Thorne's ass. The guy had some serious Mommy issues going on or something. He was constantly late for work, especially over the past two weeks, and he bragged about sleeping with more women than Lenny had fingers and toes. At first, it was amusing, but now it was damn near infuriating.

He would never talk about it, so Lenny didn't know what his deal was. He just claimed to be "having fun," and that the "old man needed to lighten up." If you had a partner that you couldn't count on, you might as well not have one at all. Hence, the reason he took the rookie, Leopold under his wing. She looked up to and respected him. She was eager to make a name for herself and move up ranks. Lenny admired her ambition, and knew without a doubt she would one day achieve her goals. She was the daughter that he and Tessa never had. A car accident had left Tessa with a broken pelvis, rendering her physically unable to carry a child to term. They had considered adoption, surrogacy, and fostering, but in the end decided that being parents was just not in the cards for them. Their only children throughout their years together came with four legs, fur, and a tail. As for Thorne, he wasn't surprised a bit that he was late, but it was unlike Leopold to not be sitting behind her desk drinking her Starbucks caramel mocha latte, thirty minutes before her shift started. She reminded Lenny of himself when he first got onto the force. Eager and ambitious. Always looking for the next case that could catapult her career.

Roaring into Seminole, Detective Shane parked his bike, and walked towards the yellow crime scene tape. There were several private citizen by standers gawking at the gruesome scene, that the uniforms had already taped off. Lenny flashed his badge, and ducked under the tape. Upon seeing him, his partner, Detective Bobby Thorne came rushing over to him.

"Hey Shane."

"Hey yourself." Lenny crossed his arms over his chiseled chest and cocked an eyebrow. "Why weren't you at the station this morning? And when the hell did you get here," Lenny asked with curiosity.

"Another wild night," Bobby said while giving a wink. "I just got here five minutes ago." Holding up his cell phone he said, "Lieutenant phoned me."

"Where's Leopold," Lenny asked, glancing around. With a look of confusion on his face, Bobby said,

"Uhhh, I don't know. Why would I know? We patrolled our area until about one in the morning, and then I dropped her back off at her place," he lied.

Looking Bobby directly in his beady blue eyes, Lenny squinted, as though thinking. He shook his head in approval, and offered a "Hmmm." Nodding over towards the body, he asked, "So what do we have?"

Crossing his arms over his chest, Bobby replied, "Female victim. She was beaten pretty badly. Mid twenties. No identification. Prepare yourself before you go over there. It's bad."

Lenny forced a small smile in appreciation for the heads up. He was a good cop. A damn good cop. There wasn't much he hadn't seen in his thirty five years on the force, and he doubted this would be any different. His partner of six months had been in the homicide division for less than five years. Still a baby as far as Lenny was concerned.

Detective Shane walked towards the victim, who was covered from head to toe in a white sheet, stained with spots of crimson red. He motioned with his arm for the CSI snapping photos to step back.

"Were you able to get photos of the shoe prints around the body, before all of these people started traipsing on my crime scene," he asked the CSI.

"I did the best I could, sir," the CSI with blonde hair said with a slight quivering in his voice. "A lot of these people were already here when I got here."

"Everyone stop," Lenny's voice boomed. All of the people working on the scene stopped in their tracks, and turned towards Detective Shane. "I want anyone who has been near this body, to get your shoe soles photographed before you leave."

Grabbing the CSI by the shoulder, Detective Shane whispered to him, "that includes law enforcement. You understand?"

"Yes, Sir."

Detective Shane sent the CSI over towards the private

citizens to snap the photos. Snapping a pair of latex gloves on, he squatted down next to the Jane Doe. Reaching for the top corner of the sheet, Lenny took a long and slow breath to brace himself for the gruesome scene that he was about to see. It was a necessary evil of being a homicide detective. His stomach was iron cast, but none the less, he never liked to see it, because what it really meant was that someone out there had lost someone they love. Possibly a wife, a mother, a daughter, a friend.

Lenny slowly peeled back the shroud. The victim was lying face down, with her head turned to the side. Her shoulder length brown tresses were matted with leaves, sand, and various outdoor debris. Bobby was right. She had suffered severe trauma about the face. Both eyes were purple and swollen shut. Lenny could tell that her nose was broken due to the offset nature of it. Dried blood from her nostrils had crusted on and around her mouth and chin. The swelling made her damn near unrecognizable. Lenny continued peeling back the covering

He moved to the victims hands to examine them. Strange. This victim had no defensive wounds to speak of, except a small abrasion on her right knuckles. This told him one of two things. Either she was restrained during the attack, or she knew her attacker and was caught off guard and didn't get a chance to react before getting the living hell beat out of her. Lenny examined her wrists for ligature marks. No signs. He then took his gloved hands and gently palpitated the area to see if there was any resistance from any sticky residue left on the skin. Bingo. Lenny smirked as he said softly, "Here's your first mistake, you son of a bitch." Moving down to her ankles, Lenny lifted her stone washed denims to check her ankles for the same residue. The victims ankles had not been restrained in the same manner. He moved to the soles of her Reebok's. Looking up at the two CSI, that were chatting off in the corner, Lenny called out like he just won the lottery, "Evidence! I need an evidence collection bag! Bring me some tweezers and some pliers too."

Peering up at Thorne who was standing over him watching his every move, Detective Shane asked, "don't you have some evidence to collect or some witness statements to take or something?"

Thorne ignored Shane's rhetorical request to get the hell away from him. "I think Detectives Wilshire and Layne have it under control," he said coolly, as he continued to loom uninvited over Detective Shane's shoulder.

Lenny reached into his pocket and popped a piece of Wrigley's into his mouth, to distract himself from punching Thorne in the ball sack. His partner or not, Thorne was really starting to get on his last nerve. Grinding the soothing spearmint gum between his molars had a calming effect on him for some reason, and he was able to refocus his energy back towards the vic.

The male CSI with the spiked blonde hair opened his evidence kit and handed the requested items to Lenny. Grasping the bag in his left, and the tweezers in his right, he lifted the victims left leg to get a better look. He could see a small round metal cylinder embedded in the vic's shoe. He grasped the edges of it and pulled. The cylinder didn't budge, and the tweezers weren't going to do the job.

Setting the tweezers down, Lenny grabbed the needle nose pliers. He had to hold the shoe on so it didn't slip off from the force at which he had to pull. The hallow metal cylinder was as big as a one inch wooden dowel.

Placing it in his hand, Lenny rolled it around and examined it. He pinched it between his thumb and index finger and rolled it between them. Raising it up to eye level, he closed one eye and examined the center. He reached for the tweezers and pulled out a tiny scroll that was the size of a fortune in a cookie.

Unwinding it, his eyes read left to right. Left to right.
Over and over again. He stood up, even though he
should have stayed on the ground to maintain his
wavering equilibrium. He couldn't believe what he
was seeing. His face grew red with anger as he gritted
his teeth. He palmed the note in his left hand so tightly,
his knuckles turned white. He closed his eyes and
moved his other hand over to his left breast pocket. His
head fell forward in regret. He should have retired six
months ago, when Tessa first brought it up. Getting his
composure once again, he unfurled the note and read it
one more time.

*Detective Shane,*
*I didn't give you the opportunity to save this one…*
*but I will give you 24 hours to save the next. Let the*
*game begin.*

Shaking his head slowly, he mumbled, "Oh God, no.
Not now." Some psycho lunatic with a hard on for him
was the last thing he needed right now. Great. Just
fucking great. There goes his official retirement
announcement, and probably his vacation with Tessa,
and probably his marriage too. Now what the hell was
he going to do? "Oh, sorry Tess, I was going to take
you on a great tropical vacation, and tell you I was
going to retire, but some psycho asshole has it out for
me, so as usual I'm putting my job first." Yeah, he
thought. That will go over like a damn lead balloon.
    He dropped the metal cylinder into the collection bag,
sealed it, and handed it to the CSI.
    Detective Lenny Shane slyly stuffed the palmed note
into the pocket of his Wranglers. It was concealing
evidence, but this one was personal. What were they
going to do? Suspend him? Take his badge? Big ass
deal. He was planning on retiring anyway. Even if they
took his pension away, he had invested his money
wisely over the years.

Had he not been so numb, he would have noticed the look of satisfaction that had spread over his partner, Bobby Thorne's face, as he turned and walked away from the body, with an ashen complexion.

# 8. MISSING

DETECTIVE Shane walked over to a private area, away from the crowd, and pulled out his cell phone, dialing Detective Leopold's number. Getting only her voicemail, he pressed the end call button without leaving a message.

He quickly dialed his Lieutenant.

"Lieutenant Whitten," she answered.

"Lieutenant," he said quickly, "have you seen or heard from Leopold yet this morning?"

"No, I haven't," she said. "I called and left her a voicemail to head out to Seminole. Why, she's not there?"

"Negative," he said. "And I don't feel good about this, Lieutenant. Thorne said he dropped her back at home last night…Do you mind if I send someone over to her house?"

"No, please do," she said. "And, Shane, keep me posted, and I'll do the same."

"Will do, Lieutenant," he said.

Stuffing his phone back into his pocket, Detective Shane approached Detectives Wilshire and Layne, and said, "have either of you seen or talked to Detective Leopold today?"

"I haven't," Detective Wilshire said.

"No, why," Detective Layne asked with concern.

"Well," Lenny said, "she's obviously not here, and no one has heard from her. Not even the Lieutenant, because I just called her to ask."

Without waiting for further instruction, Layne said, "we got this," as he tapped his partner on the shoulder, and signaled it was time for them to go.

#

Jumping into Detective Wilshire's Mercedes, Layne repeatedly dialed her digits. The first time, he left a pleading voicemail to call him, or anyone back, to let them know she was okay.

By the twentieth time, he knew he had killed all chances of ever getting with her, because she would think that he was a psycho stalker, but he didn't care. He just needed to know that she was okay, and he needed to know right now.

Detective Wilshire glanced at his partner, who was looking frazzled and frantic. "Chill out, dude," he said. "Maybe she lost her phone, or dropped it in the toilet or something."

Layne shoved his phone back into it's holster. "That doesn't explain why she wasn't at the precinct, or at the crime scene this morning," he snapped.

Wilshire nodded his head in agreement. "You got a point. Sorry, man, I'm just trying to make you feel a little better, until we can find out what's going on."

"I'm sorry too, for snapping at you," Layne said.

"I'll just feel better when we find her. She was with Thorne last night. He's shady, man,…and I don't know why, but I don't trust him. Never have."

Layne leaned over to glance at the speedometer. Wilshire was doing sixty in a forty-five. Rubbing his hand over the smooth dash, he said, "this is supposed to be a high performance car, right?"

Wilshire and Layne locked stares, as Wilshire pushed the pedal down, and accelerated to eighty five.

Layne smiled in appreciation, and eased back in his seat. "That's more like it."

Arriving at Leopold's condominium in record time, Whitten eased his Mercedes into a parking spot next to Leopold's little red smart car.

Switching the ignition off, Wilshire said, "well, her car is here."

Layne and Wilshire exited the Mercedes and approached the coral two-story building and knocked on the door marked C108.

Layne knocked aggressively and called out, "Leopold? Leopold, open up. Leopold, are you in there?"

There was no answer, so he tried the door to see if it was unlocked. No go.

Wilshire was thinking a little more clearly than Layne. "Hey partner," he nudged Layne. "Let's head to the back, and see if we have any luck there."

Both Layne and Wilshire walked to the back of the complex, to try her screened lanai door. Bingo. They walked inside the tiled screened patio, and up to the sliding glass doors. Layne tried prying at the door, but the sliders were locked as well. There was a small pet door, but both of them were way to large to fit through it.

"Son of a bitch!" Layne cursed through gritted teeth.

From their outside view through the glass sliders, they could see the length of the condo, clean through to the front door, although they could not see into the bedroom or bathroom. The place was tidy and neat. Nothing looked to be disturbed.

Layne pounded on the glass, and continued calling for her.

Wilshire watched his partner, feeling helpless. "Do you want me to find the office and get a key to her place, so we can go in," he asked.

Layne shifted on his feet, unsure of what the right call was. He wanted to know. He needed to know, but at the same time didn't want to overstep his boundaries, and invade her privacy. "What do you think," Layne asked, searching his partner's eyes for the answer.

Wilshire reassuringly clasped his hand onto Layne's shoulder. Looking him directly in the eyes, Wilshire said, "I think we need to do whatever it is we need to do, to get your mind straight. This is your call, partner. Everything looks to be in order, but if you need to go in to see for yourself, then I agree one hundred percent."

Playing with his goatee, Layne thought about it for a brief second. "Go get the key,"

Wilshire left to go find the office, as Layne paced inside the screened lanai, continuing to call her number. Pressing his ear against the glass, he did not hear her phone ringing.

Wilshire returned, and held up a shiny chrome colored key. Both he and Layne walked back around the condo to the front door.

Walking inside, Layne made a bee line for the bed and bath area. Wilshire headed for the kitchen.

Inside her room, Layne could smell the clean and fresh scent of her perfume. Her bed was made, so he looked on top of her night stands to see if there was anything of use to indicate where she was. Nothing but a lamp, an alarm clock, a pack of birth control pills, and a sappy, erotic romance novel.

Layne entered the en suite bathroom. Clicking on the light, it was as clean as the rest of the place. Reaching for the shower curtain, his heart hammered. He ripped it back in one fast swoop. Empty. Layne sighed in a heavy breath of relief. Going in for closer inspection, he noticed that there was no condensation on the curtain, in the tub, or on the tiled walls. If she did come back here last night, she didn't take a shower this morning.

Layne walked into the kitchen where Wilshire was poking around.

Holding up the clean and empty coffee pot, Wilshire said, "either she's super neat and tidy, or she wasn't here this morning. No coffee in the coffee pot. No dirty dishes in the sink, and no drying dishes."

Layne ran his hands through his long dark hair. "Yeah," he said quietly. "Beds made. No water or condensation in the bathroom from showering either."

A steel gaze settled over Layne's reddening face. "I swear to God, Wilshire. If I find out that Thorne has anything to do with this, you're going to have to arrest me for assault and battery, because I'm going to kick his skinny piece of shit ass!"

Whitten pulled his cell phone out, and started dialing. "I'll call the Lieutenant and update her. Let's get out of here." Walking towards his partner, Wilshire laid his hand reassuringly on Layne's upper bicep. "We'll figure this out, partner. We'll find her. Oh, and by the way, I couldn't arrest you, if I were your accomplice. I'd be there, right along side you."

Layne nodded in appreciation and agreement, then reluctantly sulked behind his partner, out the front door of the condo.

# 9. ESCAPE PLAN

TESSA'S eyes fluttered rapidly, as the chloroform's hold on her started to subside. Her gag reflex became initiated at her realization of the foul stench still lingering in her airways. With nausea washing over her, her saliva glands released a flood in her mouth, and she swallowed quickly and heavily. Her stomach started behaving like an involuntary muscle, tightening and heaving repeatedly, trying to spill it's contents. It was not successful. Warm and salty streams escaped her eyes, and tickled the edge of her nose.

As her consciousness fully resumed, her eyes darted around furiously in the darkness. Upon her brain registering the fact that she was bound and gagged, terror and panic spread through her like a wild fire. Her heart began to pound furiously inside her chest, and her breath came in short and fast through her dainty nose. The thumping in hear ears grew as loud as a bass drum, and a flash of internal heat consumed her entire being from her head to her toes. Her tank top quickly grew wet with perspiration between her breasts and under her arms.

Being married to a cop for thirty years, she knew that panic was not her friend in this situation. She closed her eyes and imagined Lenny's face. A calmness began to blanket her body and her mind. She could no longer feel the intense thumping in her chest cavity. She reigned in her breath, and took long, slow drags. In and out. In and out. If she were going to survive, she needed to think rationally and remain calm. She knew this, but the actual successful execution of it under the circumstances was…easier said than done.

The last thing she remembered was jamming to Aerosmith on her iPod, while developing photos in her home studio dark room. Yes… She cleaned up the breakfast dishes after Lenny left for work. Then she went into the dark room to develop some black and whites she had taken of Lenny on his new bike. She was going to pick the most artistic one and blow it up into a twenty-four by thirty-six, with a custom matte and frame, as a gift for their thirtieth anniversary. Then….She remembered hanging the photos to dry, and….. Oh, God. The memory of the struggle with the man in the ski mask came flooding into her memory. She recalled him holding something over her nose and mouth., and struggling to breathe. She didn't hear anyone enter the house or the dark room because she had her Dr. Dre Beats covering her ears.

She decided that screaming was more likely little to no use…and she definitely did not want to attract any unnecessary attention. Besides, screaming wasn't really an option with a band of duct tape running from cheek to cheek sealing her lips shut. She recognized the distinct smell of the gray tape.

Kicking or running was also not an option, as her knees were bent at a ninety degree angle. Her ankles were crossed and bound together, and by extending her fingers, she could feel a thin rope conjoining her wrists and ankles.

Her shoulders were cranked behind her beyond what would normally be comfortable, and they were starting to ache. Her right shoulder and right cheek itched and burned slightly from rubbing against the low pile carpeting beneath her. Interlocking her fingers together for leverage, she tried prying her tape bound wrists apart.

It's sticking power was unforgiving. After several failed attempts, she decided on a different approach. Using a rocking motion, she was able to maneuver herself up onto her knees. The soles of her Sketchers, made contact with the top side of her tight quarters. Her mind started racing, as claustrophobia tried to creep in. All sorts of non comforting scenarios started invading her thought process.

*Am I in some sort of makeshift coffin? Oh, God.*
*Am I buried alive? Is my air going to run out?*

With her face planted in the low pile carpet, and her arms resting on the top of her buttocks, she frantically started wiggling her shoulders and arms, like a piston. She quietly moaned in pain because of the awkward position she had to put herself in. And, her head hurt. It really hurt. That and the fact that her fingers were starting to get tingly and numb from restricted blood flow. She was making no more progress this way, than her first attempt. Being in this position did give her another thought, which sparked a glimmer of hope.

She started thinking that she was fairly flexible, because she did do yoga everyday. If she could just get her wrists over the top of her butt, then she could curl all 5'2"of her into a tight ball. Knees in close to the chest, and slip her hands over the bottom of her feet. Then her hands would be in front of her in "prayer

position." She could bend forward to get the tape off
of her mouth, then try to chew the tape off of her
wrists. If she could get that far, then getting the tape
off of her ankles as well as the rope that bound her
ankles and  wrists together would be gravy. She didn't
want to think about what would come after that. She
needed to stay focused on one step at a time.

Her thoughts were interrupted by what sounded like
footsteps. She went silent and still. Willing her ears to
hear the muffled sound of shuffling feet not far from
where she lay. Listening more intently, she heard the
creaking sound of a door closing. The slamming of it
made her jump slightly. The muffled shuffling of feet
grew louder. Closer.

It was equally terrifying as it was reassuring. If those
were footfalls, then she definitely was still above
ground. The sound grew closer and closer. Louder and
louder. There was definitely someone walking towards
her. She heard the ringing of a cell phone, just outside
of where she lay, which came to an abrupt end,
immediately followed by the sound of an object being
hurled, and shattering against the wall.

Since she hadn't yet executed her great Houdini
escape, she decided it would be better to pretend to still
be unconscious. Drawing her body in as tight as she
could get it, she used all of her strength and balance to
resume her original position. She was careful not to
make a sound. The last thing she wanted to do was to
fall over and create a loud thud, which would give
away the fact that she was awake.  She didn't choose
to play this game, but she had no choice, and since that
was the case, she would control whatever aspects of it
she could.

After what seemed to be an eternity, but in reality
probably only a minute or so, the jingle jangle of keys
split the silence. Upon hearing the sound of metal upon
metal penetration, Tessa contemplated the phrase,
"scared to death." A distinct click, pop…and a small

crack of light fled into her prison. She glanced around
wildly, and suddenly realized that she was in the trunk
of a car.

Having only seconds to peer outside of her trunk
tomb, the man in the black ski mask loomed just
outside. Her eyes were covered with darkness again, as
she closed them. Willing herself to remain calm, she
pretended to still be under a thick blanket of
unconsciousness.

Even through her neutral shade Maybelline dusted
eyelids, the fluorescent light filtered through them with
the trunk now fully open. In her mind she kept
chanting, "Lenny, please find me. Lenny, please find
me. Please find me before it's too late."

She could tell her captor was standing directly in
front of her, when the brighter light filtering through
her lids dimmed slightly. Even though her eyes
remained sealed shut, she could tell her captor was the
man in the ski mask, because of his smell. Her
olfactory recognized his distinct smell of pine mixed
with English Leather. She had smelled the same scent
on him, before he put that white cloth on her face. He
roughly grabbed her arm and pulled her towards
himself, causing her cheek to become even more rug
burned.

Panic seizing her brain made her want to do
something…anything, to get the hell out of this
predicament. But what? There was nothing for her to
do, other than be at the mercy of this lunatic.

She started thinking that he obviously didn't want to
kill her, or she would already be dead. Common sense
said that he was taking her somewhere, or was she
already there? Otherwise, why put her in the trunk of a
car? But why? Was he kidnapping her? Was he taking
her somewhere else to kill her?

Being on her stomach, with her head towards the
man, she peered out with her right eye. It was towards
the carpet, and the hair falling over her face would

offer good enough cover for her not to get caught. She kept her left eye closed.

Tessa could make out that he was thin and lanky. He was wearing the same get up that he was wearing earlier. All black. Black pants, black t-shirt, blue latex gloves, and a black ski-mask. She couldn't identify her attacker, because his features were hiding behind the mask. There was something that was familiar about him, but it escaped her. The only thing she knew for sure was that he was a thin and wiry white male....and he had a gun strapped onto his right hip. A Beretta? She couldn't get a good enough look.

*He's going to shoot me in the back right here in this trunk, then dump my body somewhere,* she thought.

She watched as he started moving his hand towards his right hip, but she couldn't bear to witness him unsheathe it. She was already in a state of torture, knowing she was taking her last breaths.

She closed her open eye, and whispered a silent prayer. She prayed that it would be quick, and that she wouldn't suffer. She also prayed for her Husband. She knew that he would fly off the rails. He would turn in his badge, which she wanted him to do, but not because he was trading it in for the life of a revenge bent renegade mercenary. His mind would snap and he would become the Special Ops soldier she met so long ago. She just prayed that he could accept the facts of life and be able to live out the rest of his days in peace. She knew the chances of that were slim to none, but she could still pray for it.

In her silent prayer, she barely noticed the tugging on the rope that laced her wrists and ankles together. She heard a sawing noise. To her surprise, the man in the mask had cut the rope, and freed her bondage. She let her legs freefall limply.

"This is going to be so much fun," he said in a maniacal tone.

He closed the trunk, again sealing Tessa in darkness.

She heard the car door open, and the engine roar to life. She heard the distinct sound of an electric garage door opening in the closed space. She blinked slowly, and thanked whoever was listening, that she was still breathing.

As she felt the car roll in motion, she wasted no time. She not only felt the vibration of the road, but the entire car was vibrating with bass. The man either had an obvious kinship with rap music, or was just using it to mask her possible screams, so that no one would hear her.

With the rope now cut, She made quick work of slipping her hands over her butt and getting them in front of her body. She reached up and slowly started working the sticky gag from her lips. As the tape pulled on her skin, and peeled free from her face, she took a deep breath through her mouth, and did a facial calisthenics routine. The tape around her ankles was wound around several times. She felt around and picked desperately at it, but couldn't find the start or end of the tape What was she thinking? That it was just going to peel it off like a banana peel? She painstakingly had to rip piece by piece. Little by little, the tape was coming off in small strips.

Completely freeing herself from the sticky shackles, Tessa moved her open palms around the trunk floor. She was searching for something. Anything. *A tire iron would be nice,* she thought. After working the entire area, her hands came upon the slim rope that was used to tie her ankles and wrists together. She flung the rope out of her grasp, like a child throwing a temper tantrum. She immediately regretted it, as an idea hatched. She frantically felt around in the darkness to find her one and only string of hope.

In the darkness, a spark of victory consumed her, as she felt the nylon rope beneath her fingertips. Grasping it with her outstretched fingers, she pulled it in, and balled it in her hand. Tessa maneuvered her body in the

trunk, so that her head was facing towards the front
of the car. With her left hand, she grasped the nylon
loop that was sewn onto the back of the rear split
bench seat. Using her right hand, she pushed on the
seat, trying to disengage the seat lock. If she could get
the seat to fold down, she could crawl out of the trunk
and into the rear passenger seat. She had several failed
attempts at gently nudging on the seat. A raw emotion
surged through her, and she palm punched the seat
with force. She cringed as a loud pop echoed through
the trunk. She held onto that nylon loop like it was her
only lifeline, keeping the seat in its upright position.
She decided it would be a good idea to wait a few
minutes in case the driver heard the noise. She lay
there barely breathing, with her ears on high alert.

The throbbing music changed into another bass
pounding tune. Being that he didn't pull the car over,
and he didn't turn the stereo down, Tessa decided it
was now or never.

Closing her eyes, she very slowly inched the seat
back down. Inch by inch. It didn't make a sound, at
least not one that was audible over the pounding bass
speaker. With the seat back extended all the way down,
Tessa got up on her elbows and used her forearms to
painstakingly inch her way out of the trunk. With her
body halfway out behind the drivers seat, she kept her
head down, but looked around. It was late afternoon,
but she had no idea what time it was, or how long she
had been out. All that she could see of the driver
through the rear view mirror, was the top of his head.
He had very short hair. Buzzed hair.

Slithering her legs completely out of the trunk, she
kneeled and sat on the soles of her feet, in the back
seat. Crouching down in position, she took the rope
and wound it a couple of times around each of her
trembling hands. The driver was completely oblivious
to her presence.

Taking several deep breaths, she gave herself a small

pep talk. As she raised up, her sapphire eyes met
with the surprised look in his icy blues, in the rearview
mirror. In a quick jump rope move, Tessa swung the
rope over the headrest and the man's head, coming to
settle in the crook of his neck. Kicking her feet from
beneath her, she firmly planted her soles on the back of
the driver's seat as she leaned back and pulled, as hard
as her quaking body would let her.

Her hands became bright red, as the rope cut into
them. The Lincoln started swerving all over the tree
lined road, as the driver started to lose consciousness,
and control of the vehicle. Her body swayed with the
momentum of the barreling steel as it went left to right,
swerving all over the nearly deserted road. With a
sudden jarring impact, she was thrown to the passenger
side of the car, causing her hands to lose grip on the
rope. Immediately following the collision, the ear
piercing pitch of grinding metal rang through the car as
it did a dance with a guardrail. Glancing out the
window, Tessa saw the warm glow of sparks flying
everywhere. She heard a loud bang, and the car went
into a tailspin.

Hanging on for dear life, she wrapped her arms
around the passenger side head rest, as the car spun
around and around. Her dizziness was interrupted
when the side of her head smashed into the passenger
rear window.

The swirling black Lincoln crashed through the chain
link fence that lined the entirety of the Alley, and came
to rest against an Australian Pine. Battered and broken,
it's engine simmered with white smoke billowing from
below the hood.

Bobby Thorne had had both arms resting on the
steering wheel of the battered Lincoln, with his head
tucked neatly in between. Turning his face to the rear
seat, he saw that Tessa was slumped in the backseat.
Down for the count, for the second time today. He took
a moment to rub the front of his neck, and check it out

in the mirror. His Adam's apple was bright red, but other than that, there wasn't a distinct ligature mark running horizontally across the width of it. He turned the ignition key, but the engine made only a clicking sound. He hastily made several more attempts in quick succession to get the engine to turn over, but it refused.

"Fuck! Fuck! Fuck!," he exclaimed, as he pounded his fists on the steering wheel. This was not part of the plan. He was awestruck at the fight this little bitch had in her. He was going to have to come up with something quick, if he wanted this to go a little more smoothly when she woke up. He quickly surmised that his only option was to proceed on foot.

Snapping his duffle up off of the passenger seat, he exited the car, leaving the door wide open.

There were no other cars in the immediate area, but he could see some headlights approaching in the distance of the flat, split highway, from the same direction he had just come. He set the duffle on the trunk lid, and returned to the open driver's side door. Grabbing her by the feet, he hastily maneuvered Tessa's limp body out of the back seat, and pulled her up into the front. Sliding her out of the door, he slung her over his shoulder like a sack of potatoes. Her dead weight wasn't enough to slow his stride. He slung his duffle over his other shoulder, and took one last look at the crumpled metal, and kicked the rear quarter panel. "Fucking piece of shit!"

As the approaching headlights grew larger, he estimated they were several miles in the distance. He needed to get out of here before anyone spotted him. With any luck, they wouldn't be a rubber-necker, and just keep on driving. He jogged off of Alligator Alley, into the thick cover of the Everglades, with Tessa's body flapping like a leaf in a windstorm.

# 10. BAD NEWS

LIEUTENANT Sara Whitten sat at her desk, and glanced up at the clock. The hands were at four-fifteen. Sitting there in a trance, with her eyes fixed on the second hand, her mind ticked along with it.

Feeling at a complete loss of direction, she let her mind wander. She subconsciously tapped her pen on the desk, to the beat of the second hand. Snapping out of it, she picked up a copy of this mornings crime scene report, and started to read it again.

Hearing a soft knock on her door, she looked up, and motioned Manny Sanchez, Head of the Forensics Department, to come in.

Manny closed the door behind him, and pulled the shades. He turned to her with a solemn look on his face.

Setting down the case file, she asked, "What? "What is it, Manny?"

Manny loosened the knot of his slim purple tie. Clearing his throat, he said, "I don't know how to tell you this, Sara."

Lieutenant Whitten didn't like the sound of Manny's voice. She closed her eyes briefly. "Tell me what," she asked apprehensively.

Manny stuffed his hands into his slacks. He hung his head, and diverted his eyes to the floor for longer than a quick glance. Slowly bringing them back up to reconnect with Sara's, he said, "The Jane Doe, from this morning?"

"Yes?"

"I ran her fingerprints through my database, and I don't need to wait on getting a positive ID from the Medical Examiner...Sara,... it's a positive I.D for Detective Kate Leopold." Manny clasped both of his hands over his mouth, as if he couldn't believe what had just come out of it.

Lieutenant Sara Whitten felt the air get sucked out of her lungs. She remained seated behind her desk in her plush chair, with her mouth agape, but unable to form any words.

# 11. BLIND SIDED

LENNY left the station early that Friday afternoon at four o'clock, with nothing to go on, but a bad feeling. When he left, the station had not heard back from the Medical Examiner, regarding any clues, identity, or findings on the Jane Doe, and Kate Leopold was MIA. His mind had raced all day, trying to think of who would be after him. The problem was, there were way too many. In a thirty-five year long career, he had put away a lot of scumbags. The obvious choice was last night's un-apprehended escaped convict, Robert Verde, but it just didn't seem to fit. For one thing, Verde just broke out of prison the night of the murder.

Assuming he in fact busted out of the pen, made his way across the Alley, over from Miami, and was able to locate a victim, the crime scene just didn't fit his style.

Serial killers usually formed a bond with a certain type of killing ritual. Usually. Maybe the twenty years in the pen changed things for him? Maybe he was rushed, and just wanted to commit the act, without caring about the how?

As the warm tropical air whipped his silver hair around, the typical Florida sunshine was giving way to dark thunderclouds. A low rumbling loomed off in the distance, as Lenny cranked the throttle down. He was devising plan B, since the Mexican Riviera trip, and the badge retirement would now have to wait. He figured a nice dinner and a trip to the jewelry store with ladies choice should do the trick. The trip wasn't scheduled for another three weeks, but unless they got a lucky break in the case, it would probably take longer to find the pen wielding psycho. Hopefully not, since it was made clear that there would be another victim within 24 hours. Considering he was wanting to play some type of sick game with Lenny personally, retirement was not a current option.

Lenny decided to not even mention his "plan A" gift to Tessa. He didn't want to break her heart twice. And, he definitely didn't want to tell her why he had to go to plan B. She would just be worried about him more than usual. With his career in law enforcement, it was hard enough for her to see him walk out the door and not know if he would ever walk back in it. Even though she didn't actually bring it up, he knew there was more than once that she contemplated divorcing him. Not because she didn't love him, but because she did. Too much. To tell her that he was player # 2 in some type of demented game would just be cruel and unusual punishment. She deserved better than that., and he would definitely be a divorcee if he told her. Not happening. He would just as soon take a bullet.

Lenny cruised past the Spanish Mediterranean houses

on Palm Drive. He pulled into the only one on the street that had bougainvillea growing on a trellis, just as big fat summer raindrops started to spatter on the concrete. He pulled his bike, that had gotten a minimal wash from nature, into the garage next to his '67 Mustang. It was a two car garage, but currently held only a restored black cherry 67' Mustang with a Cobra 427 Jet, nine inch posse rear end, and some sexy M15's. She had all the trimmings. It could easily turn 11's in a quarter mile. It was his Father's baby, but he inherited it, and loved it even more than his bike. If his Dad could see it now, he would be proud. Lenny had put a lot of labor and a whole lot more love into it. Money too, but he didn't care about that. It was how he held on to the memory of his dearly departed, and honored his memory by occasionally taking her to the quarter mile track to open up some whoop ass. Walking in through the side door, the house was eerily quiet.

"Tessa? Tess, I'm home," he called out while raiding the refrigerator for a Budweiser. He definitely needed a drink after today. He wanted tonight to be special, and his mind to be there with Tessa, not somewhere else….like on trying to figure out who the lunatic was that wrote him a personal note and left it with a dead body.

He popped the cap off of the brown translucent bottle, and took a long swig of the amber liquid. Hearing no response, he went in search of her.

Figuring she must be in her darkroom, he walked down the hall, looking into each of the rooms. Each one empty.

Approaching the darkroom door, Lenny noticed something smeared on the white tile. Bending down he poked his middle finger into it and rubbed it with his thumb. His eyes widened at the sight of its crimson color. Blood? His cop instincts took over. He set his bottled beer onto the floor, and undid the safety on his

Colt M45.

He called out once more in a louder voice, "Tessa, are you home?" Tessa didn't answer his call.

Hearing nothing but silence, he slid the weight of his Colt M45 pistol out of his shoulder harness, and was ready to use it.

Standing with his back flat against the wall, just outside of the darkroom door, he knocked three times on the door. Maybe she was listening to her iPod and just didn't hear him?

With his gun in his right hand, he reached the door handle with his left. Flinging the door open, it banged and ricocheted off the opposing wall. He led into the room, arm extended. Cocked and ready.

Seeing the room was empty, Lenny was utterly confused. He holstered his gun, and ran his hand over his thick salt and pepper mustache, while his quick adrenaline rush subsided. This case was going to have him on edge until they put the asshole behind bars. Maybe he would have something a little stiffer, and a little more relaxation inducing than beer over dinner. Maybe a couple of stiff Jack and coke's would do the trick. He nodded his head in approval at the thought.

Inspecting the room more closely, he walked towards the long metal work table, and bent to pick up some rolls of film, and Tessa's Nikon camera, that lay on the floor. This just wasn't right. Tessa took very good care of her equipment, and would never leave her camera sitting around, especially on the floor. Picking them up, he set them back up on the long steel table. His stomach twisted in knots at the sight of a memory stick, that had a note attached to it. *17 hours*, was all it said. A number and one word was all it took to send him over the edge.

Lenny's nostrils flared as he roared, "You son of a bitch!" In his fit of rage, he wanted to grab the metal table and tip it over in a deafening clatter, and punch a few holes into the wall. Slamming his fists on the cold table, he got himself under control. Trashing the crime scene would only compromise it. Cop or not, when he found this bastard that took his wife, he was going to plug him like a leaky sink.

After his initial outburst, Lenny knew that he couldn't let his emotions get the better of him. A level head and a clear mind were the only things that would help him save Tessa. Against all hope, he took out his iPhone and dialed Tessa's number, with shaky hands. Pacing around the room, the time in between the rings felt like an eternity. He longed to hear her sweet voice on the other end. Getting her voicemail, in a reassuring tone he said, "Tessa, honey, I love you. If you get this message, please call me if you can. I know that you've been abducted. I WILL find you. I love you. Don't ever forget that. Keep fighting. For me. For us." Lenny hit the end call button in hesitation. He wanted to call her again, just to hear her voice, but knew that he was on a time clock. He needed to get moving. Now.

He exited the darkroom, sticking the memory stick in his vest pocket. He stopped outside the door to grab his beer, and chugged it down in four big gulps. Walking through the kitchen, he tossed the bottle into the plastic recycle bin, and walked out the side door to the garage.

Hurrying over to his large red Snap On tool box, his unsteady hands fumbled to unclip his keys from his belt loop. The reality of what was happening slammed into him, like a sledgehammer. The keys rattled as he tried to isolate the right one. He was out of sorts. Normally he was Mr. Cool, Calm, and Collected. He couldn't lose Tessa. She was his rock. The woman behind the man.

Steadying the key, and unlocking the tool box, he opened the large bottom drawer. He glanced over the small arsenal of fire arms and other weapons he kept. Trying to decide what to take was too much of a decision. He hastily grabbed a large camo print duffle bag from a nearby shelving unit that he kept packed

with outdoor essentials for camping trips. He dumped
the entire drawer's contents into the bag. His eyes did a
quick scan around the garage for anything else he
might need, when he noticed the broken remnants of
what used to be a cell phone, lying on the far edge of
the garage floor. Inspecting it closer, he saw that it was
Tessa's. His only link to her, or her to the rest of the
world, smashed. Useless.

He removed his keys from the toolbox, secured them
back onto his belt loop, and hurried back into the
house.

Jogging into the master bedroom, he threw the camo
duffle bag on the damask striped king sized sleigh bed.
His boots clicked across the floor as he walked over to
the white washed armoire. He grabbed several changes
of clothes and stuffed them in the bag.

Hoisting the bag up onto his shoulder, he hurried
back into the kitchen. Lying the bag on the cool marble
top, he grabbed a pen and notepad from the junk
drawer, and scribbled:

*Sara,*
*The body we found today at Seminole was no*
*accident. The first note, I found on the body. The*
*second note was left for me at home. He has Tessa.*
*There is blood in the hallway, and I know for sure that*
*he was in the darkroom, so make sure you dust for*
*prints. I am going after him. I also need to know the*
*identity of the Seminole vic as soon as you hear from*
*the ME to see if we can narrow down a list of suspects-*
*Lenny*

Lenny stuffed the note into an envelope, along with
the two notes that had been left for him, and left it lay
on the counter. He had no evidence, but he would bet
his right arm that the MIA Detective Kate Leopold was
not just a coincidence. He didn't want to think that the
vic from this morning could be her, but he couldn't

ignore the mounting signs. He didn't think it would be a good idea to leave his thoughts about that in the note to his Lieutenant, so he let it be. He sealed the envelope and scribbled *Lieutenant Sara Whitten* on the front of it. He removed his police issued gun from his shoulder holster, and laid it on top of the note. He had plenty of government issued unregistered replacements in his duffle. Compliments of his Special Ops days.

Lenny hoisted his duffle into the passenger side seat of the Mustang. He pulled the car out into the paved driveway, and locked the doors. He jogged across the street to Mr. Perkins' house, with the slowly falling raindrops plinking off of his wraparound sunglasses, that were sitting on top of his head. With any luck, Mr. Perkins would be home, and not nosing around the neighborhood.

Lenny opted not to ring the doorbell, and wrapped on the door in a continuous motion. Peering through the wall of windows on the porch, he saw the plump man shuffling towards the door. Mr. Perkins opened the door with a smile on his face.

"Well, hello there," Mr. Perkins said jovially. "Looks like were going to get some rain," he said while glancing up at the sky.

Having no time for small talk, Lenny said in an anxious tone, "Hi, Mr. Perkins. Listen, did you see anything out of the ordinary today?"

Rubbing the top of his half bald head, he asked quizzically, "You mean besides the company you had this morning?"

"I didn't have company this morning," Lenny said matter of factly.

"Why you most certainly did. I was swinging on the porch here," Mr. Perkins motioned to the white wicker porch swing. " I was reading the morning paper about 7:30, like I always do, when I saw a black car pull out of your garage...and it wasn't that beauty over there," Mr. Perkins stated while pointing over to the Mustang.

With hope rising in his voice, Lenny asked, "Did you get a license plate number?"

Pushing his square rimmed glasses up on his round face, Mr. Perkins replied, "Nope. Nope, sure didn't. But it was a black car. Black car. Sedan type. Four doors with dark windows."

"Did you see who was driving the car? Was it a man, a woman, two men?"

"Nope. Didn't see who it was. Windows were too dark."

Hanging his head, Lenny said, "Thanks for your help, Mr. Perkins. Another police officer will probably be over to see you in a little while. Her name is Lieutenant Whitten. If you remember anything else at all, be sure and tell her."

"Is everything all right," Mr. Perkins called to Lenny as he abruptly left the porch and ran towards the Mustang.

Lenny held his hand up in a stiff wave to Mr. Perkins as the wheels of the Mustang laid rubber on his paved driveway.

Grabbing his cell, he speed dialed his Lieutenant. He left Sara an urgent voicemail explaining that she needed to get over to his house, and check the kitchen island countertop. He apologized that he didn't have time to explain, and that everything would make sense once she got to his house.

Lenny ended the call, and his next was to his partner, Bobby Thorne. In frustration, Lenny wondered why the hell wasn't anyone answering their phones? He left a voicemail for Thorne to call him immediately. He didn't necessarily want or need his help, he just wanted to know where he was.

With his track record, he didn't expect Thorne to call him back. It was after all a Friday afternoon, and Lenny was sure that Thorne was already out having his usual weekend fun that seemed to overflow into the weekdays. He was damn sure going to talk to Sara about this one after this was all over. He didn't want anyone else on his team getting stuck with Thorne after he left the force. Particularly Leopold, that is if she were still alive, or Layne, or Wilshire, or anyone else, for that matter.

Speeding southbound on US 41, Lenny whipped the Mustang into the nearest Walgreens parking lot. Grabbing the memory stick, he strode through the electronic doors as though his ass was on fire. Having little to no patience, he continuously slapped the bell on the counter at the photo center. A kid with greasy black hair and turtle shell glasses rushed behind the counter.

"Yes sir," the kid stated, not asked, because he could feel the no bullshit vibe that Lenny was unintentionally giving off.

Pulling the memory stick out of his front vest pocket, he held it up and asked, "how long?"

Pointing to the sign in the photo center behind him, the kid asked "One hour photo is available?"

Shaking his head, "not gonna do," Lenny said, as he opened his vest, and flashed his badge. "This here is emergency life and death evidence kid. You're not that busy, so I'm going to ask you once again. How long?"

Wringing his hands, the kid nervously looked around. He didn't really pay too much attention to the badge, but got an eyeful of the gun that the guy on the other side of the counter was packing.

With his voice cracking, the kid in the Walgreens uniform said, "If you want to wait, I can have them developed in about fifteen minutes?"

He hoped that this would be a good enough answer.

Handing the small black gadget over to the kid, Lenny said, "Make it quicker if you can, but do not mess these photos up," he warned. "I'll wait right here," Lenny said, while tapping his pointer finger on the photo counter.

With a shaking hand, the kid took the memory stick, and the threat seriously.

About five minutes into the wait, Lenny realized that he did not have his cell phone. Watching the employee working diligently on getting the photos processed, Lenny called to him, "hey kid, I'll be right back. I gotta run out to my car."

Reaching into the Mustang, he retrieved his iPhone, and saw the missed call light blinking. Dialing his voicemail, he entered his four digit code, and waited.

"Lenny, hi. It's your Lieutenant, Sara. Listen, I don't know exactly what in the hell is going on, but I have some news for you that I would rather not give you over the phone, regarding our Jane Doe this morning. I got your message earlier, and I'm at your place now. In light of that, I'm calling to tell you that there is a suspicious vehicle…a dark sedan, on Alligator Alley that has been in an accident, but there are no visible passengers around anywhere. It could be a lead. I'm going to finish up here, and see if I get a lead on anything else that will help us bring Tessa home. Lenny, whoever this bastard is, he's crazy. Be careful."

Lenny hit the end button, and decided that the Jane Doe information the Lieutenant had for him could wait. He already knew who it was in his gut anyway, but didn't want to admit it to himself. Hearing it from her would just make it all too real. He walked back into the store up to the photo counter, where the kid looked ten shades of white.

Handing Lenny the envelope, the kid swallowed hard with saucer eyes and said, "No charge, sir."

Lenny gave the kid a nod, and said, "thanks, kid."

Settling behind the wheel of the Mustang, Lenny opened the envelope and took out the photos.

He started flipping through them at a furious pace. His heart sank to the pit of his stomach, as the photos revealed Detective Kate Leopold, as beautiful as he had known her. A gruesome chronicle of her becoming the unrecognizable Jane Doe from this morning. He wanted to stop looking at the photos, but continued on. After Kate's last photo, there were pictures of his Tessa. The photos depicted her gagged and tied, with a black and blue gash on her forehead, laying just outside her darkroom, on the hallway floor of their home.

He had no need to call Sara now. He knew the news she was going to tell him. His instincts had been right. First his Katy, now his Tessa.

Pinching the bridge of his nose, he let his head slump forward, to rest on top of the steering wheel. He could barely catch his breath, as he sat there and shook while he sobbed. Finally gathering himself, he wiped the hot tears from his bloodshot eyes, and the snot dripping from his nose. Reaching into his back pocket, he hastily popped a piece of Wrigley's to calm his nerves, although he could have gone for a shot or two of Jack. Reaching over into the glove box, he pulled out a red and blue flasher, which he never had use for until now. Setting it up on the dash, he flipped it on, siren and all. He fired up the Mustang, and did a burnout in the Walgreens parking lot, leaving nothing but a trail of white billowing smoke, and the smell of burning hot rubber.

The weight of his foot pushed the pedal to it's limit. The Mustang's engine roared to life as he took off like a bullet. He sped down US 41 towards the Alley so fast, that everything was nothing but a blur.

# 12. DECEPTION

UNDER the Everglade's dark canopy, Bobby Thorne shed his mask. He no longer needed it. It was now dark out, but there were also other reasons. He was deliberate in leaving a trail that his partner, Detective Shane could follow. He wanted to make it easy, but not too easy. He was the spider that was spinning a web to lure his prey right into his trap.

He was methodical in setting up some booby type traps that would hinder Detective Shane's progress, but only in a temporary way. He actually wanted Detective Shane to find him and his beloved Tessa. Only when the time was right, though. This was his game, his rules. Checkmate would only happen when he was ready, and all of the pieces of his plan had come together.

He had left Tessa tied to a tree, so she would be going nowhere fast. Besides, when he left her, she was still out like a light. She looked so peaceful sleeping there with the campfire flickering about, like a million candles illuminating her soft features. Make no false mistake, thoughtfulness was not the reason why he lit the campfire. There were dangerous creatures out here. Alligators, panthers, bears, and snakes, just to name a few. She was his prey, not theirs, so he would keep them at bay with fire. Little did she know, none of those predators were as dangerous as he.

The hardest part of his plan was over now. Yes, he had suffered minor setbacks, but his plan was back on track. He had the girl, and the bait would follow. The rest would be gravy. He was almost saddened at the thought. All of the years of planning, coming to an end. He was definitely looking forward to the look on Detective Shane's face... watching him feel the same agony and rage that he had caused all of those years ago. He would then see what it felt like. Unfortunately, he wouldn't be around to see Detective Layne's face when he found out that he would never see his precious Kate again. Damn.

Hearing the sound of rustling brush far off the distance, snapped Bobby Thorne out of his daydream state. He finished tying off the trip wire he had laid, and covered it up with forest floor debris.

It was time to switch to Mr. Nice Guy, and go wake up the sleeping princess. And, it would be a whole lot easier to get on the move, if she were to unknowingly cooperate. He wanted Detective Shane close, but not too close. Not just yet.

# 13. A HERO

CROAKING frogs, chirping crickets, hooting birds, and various other sounds of nature invaded Tessa's ears. She shook her head to ward off the annoying buzz of mosquitoes that were relentlessly dive bombing her. She would give almost anything to have some Off bug repellant right now. The flickering campfire was the only light source under the thick canopy. She sat on a blanket of dried pine needles, with her legs extended in front of her. The rear side of her sweatpants were damp, where the moist ground beneath had permeated through the dry topped pine straw. A light moan escaped her lips, when she realized the pounding headache that was invading her skull. She noticed through slightly blurred vision, that her ankles and wrists were no longer bound, but that damn nylon rope was wound around her torso, securing her to a tree. And she thought wearing an under wire bra was uncomfortable. Heaving her midsection forward, she tried loosening the rope in order to slip out. She was getting nowhere fast.

The man in the mask was no where in sight. Peering around, her environment looked the same in all directions. Trees. Lots and lots of trees, and a campfire. When was this awful nightmare going to end? One thing was for sure, if she did make it out of this alive, she, nor Lenny for that fact, would never forget their 30th anniversary. Like ever.

She heard the soft crunching of leaves not too far off into the distance. Jesus, it could be a black bear, or a panther out here. She couldn't decide if it would be better or worse than seeing her captor again. She decided that if it were him, she would face him head on. She was tired of being scared, tired of the days events, and wanted to know what the hell this was all about. She resolved to asking bluntly when he showed his face again.

Drawing in a deep breath, she made out a dark and shadowy figure closing in from the distance. The dried out palm fronds crunched under his feet. Her anger turned into relief as the approaching face was illuminated by the flickering camp fire.

"Oh, thank God," Tessa exclaimed. A smile lit up her face from ear to ear, as she recognized Lenny's partner. Although she didn't know him that well, she had met him once or twice before, at one of the Department's family cookouts.

Detective Bobby Thorne put his finger to his lips, indicating to Tessa to keep it quiet. Holstering his gun and looking around, he started trying to undo the rope that was keeping Tessa sequestered to the tree.

"Where is he," he asked in a whisper.

"I don't know," she panted. "Please. Just hurry. There should be a knife in that backpack over there," she rattled out quickly. "Please, Bobby, get me out of here," she pleaded.

Running over to the backpack, Detective Bobby Thorne rifled through it until he found the hunting knife, that he already knew was there. Going behind the tree, he started sawing through the layers of rope.

Hearing far off footfalls closing in on the distance, Thorne started working faster, and sweat beaded on his brow in the thick humidity. Tessa closed her eyes and started moving her silent lips in prayer.

Feeling the last restraint loosen, Tessa scrambled up off of the ground. She stood too quickly, and had to grip the tree to steady herself. Feeling extremely light headed, she stood there, thankful that the tree was there to lean on.

Lightly grasping her under the armpit, Detective Thorne tried to steady her on her own two feet. "Are you okay? Do you need help walking?"

She nodded in response, as her eyes grew large with panic. He was almost there. She needed to get away. Now. Detective Thorne grabbed her by the arm, and together they jogged off into the brush.

Grabbing the backpack on the way out, Detective Thorne swung it around his shoulders. It bobbed up and down on his back, in rhythm with his and Tessa's light jog.

About ten feet into the dense brush, Detective Thorne pulled his police issued flash light out of his belt holster, to illuminate their path. Keeping up the quick pace made Tessa want to vomit. She feared that she may have a concussion. Not to mention the fact that she had not eaten since breakfast, and had been knocked out twice today. From what she could remember, anyway. She was already a little unsteady on her feet, and the debris littered ground wasn't exactly smooth.

Doubling over with a pain in her side, Detective Thorne offered her assistance.

"I need to rest, Bobby. My head hurts so bad, and I'm starving."

"Okay," he said understandingly. "Let's see if we have anything here for you."

He removed the backpack off of his shoulders and placed it on the ground. Using his flashlight to peer through it, he pulled out a chocolate chip granola bar, and a bag of peanuts. Handing them to her, he asked, "can you eat them while we keep moving?"

"Sure," she said, rubbing her sore head. Her face grew quizzical and then asked, "Bobby,... why are we running? You're a cop." Pointing towards his belt she said, "You have a gun."

"I do. And I am a cop, but I also have no backup. I don't know who or what I'm up against, and my first priority is not to apprehend the suspect, but to protect you, and get you out of here. If I confront him, and something happens to me, where does that leave you? We need to keep ahead of him. Now, can you eat that while we keep moving?"

Tessa nodded her head in approval, as she and Detective Thorne continued to move further and deeper into the brush.

# 14. THE HUNT IS ON

FIGURING he had no other leads right at the moment, Lenny decided to check out the suspicious car that was found on the Alley, that Lieutenant Sara Whitten had phoned him about. Even if she hadn't phoned him about it, his talk with Mr. Perkins confirmed that there was a black sedan outside his house this morning. Whether or not it was the same sedan, remained to be seen. Regardless, it would have been his next stop anyway. Knowing Lieutenant Whitten was already processing anything left at the scene in his house, he would make good use of his time until, or if she called him with any other leads.

Barreling down the highway, he kept one hand on the steering wheel, and the other on the Hurst shifter, prepared to downshift, or blare the horn if necessary.

Even with his body vibrating from the raw power that

his car was unleashing, he maneuvered the Mustang
through the traffic with ease. With the siren blaring,
and the red and blue whirling light, he didn't bother to
stop at the toll booth. He veered into the Sun Pass lane
and blew right through that bitch.

After twenty five minutes of his M15'S pounding the
pavement at a buck twenty, he noticed a set of freshly
laid skid marks on the road. Lenny slowed the beastly
Cobra 427 Jet, down to a mere fifty. It made him feel
like an Olympic sprinter with a twisted ankle. The
guardrail to his right was a mangled mess of steel,
which Lenny followed to it's end.

Looking past the guardrail and the broken fence,
Lenny saw the battered remnants of a black sedan,
which had come to rest against a tree. Her crumpled
remnants made it obvious that she was going nowhere
fast.

Pulling the Mustang on to the right shoulder of the
road, he kept the flasher on, but silenced the ear
piercing siren. Before stepping out of the vehicle, he
flipped on his hazard lights, because dusk was setting
in. The dry grass crunched beneath his boots, as he
followed the mowed down path of the thick brush with
his flashlight, to where the black Lincoln Continental
had come to it's resting place.

His gut was telling him that this car was the same
sedan that Mr. Perkins had told him he had saw leaving
his driveway earlier this morning. He just wanted to
find some type of confirmation. Grabbing his iPhone,
Lenny snapped a picture of the license plate, and sent it
to Lieutenant Sara Whitten. He was hoping that
running the plate would give him a clue as to whom he
was dealing with.

To keep his own prints from contaminating a
potential crime scene, Lenny slipped on some outdoor
type gloves he had removed from his camo duffle.
Pulling open the driver's side door of the Lincoln, an
intense blast of heat pressed down on him. The hot

Florida sun had a way of making the inside of a sealed up car feel like an oven on high. The distinct smell of pine freshener and English Leather was way overpowering, and rolled out of the car like a thick fog. He clicked the glove box open, to reveal nothing but an empty vessel.

"Shit," he exclaimed, as he slammed the empty vessel back to its closed position. Of course the damn car registration was not in there. That would make his life way to easy.

Noticing that curiously, the driver's side back seat was flipped down, he pulled the trunk release lever, and went around to the back of the car to peer inside.

Lenny's heart skipped a couple of beats when he saw the scattered remnants of crumpled duct tape strewn throughout the trunk. Flashes of Katy's battered and broken body flashed through his mind. The thought of Tessa being hurt like that was unimaginable. Just the thought of it made him sick. Literally. Bracing himself with one hand on the trunk of the car, and the other on his knee, Lenny littered the grass with the remnants of his last meal. After his stomach calmed down, he wiped his mouth, and popped a piece of Wrigley's. Slowly swallowing the spearmint flavor from the thin stick of gum, he got his bearings back. He made a conscious decision to not let his mind go there again. If all he got done was puking, then he would be burying Tessa right along side Katy. He had to release the emotional attachment, and follow this case just like any other. Continuing to inspect the trunk, Lenny noticed that there was a small blood stain on the carpet, but nothing that was life threatening. Picking up the pieces of duct tape to inspect them more closely, he saw one long strand of golden blonde hair. He would be willing to bet his left arm that it belonged to Tessa. He was also willing to bet that it would be a forensic match to the tape residue found on Katy's wrists.

In his mind he started to create a picture. Tessa is

restrained in the trunk of the car. She somehow
manages to remove all of her restraints, and enters the
vehicle by flipping down the driver's side back
passenger seat. Then what? She and the driver engage
in a struggle. The driver loses control of the car, and
crashes into a tree. Where the hell were they? Did they
get picked up by someone, or ....

Lenny turned, and looked off into the thick expanse
of the Everglades. He scanned the tree line for
movement. Nothing but still trees. Moving his eyes
closer to where he stood, Lenny inspected the ground
and the surrounding area of the vehicle for tracks. Sure
as shit, there was one fresh set of large footprints,
broken twigs, and bent grass leaving a breadcrumb trail
straight into the Everglades. He would have noticed
them when he was looking at the ground before, had
his mind been where it was supposed to be. At the
time, it was on a one way futile effort to keep his food
where it belonged.

Walking back to the Mustang, he turned off both sets
of flashing lights, and stuffed the keys into his pocket.
Before setting off, he grabbed his duffle, and slung it
over his shoulder. Daylight and time were your best
friend when you were tracking an animal, and he was
quickly running out of both.

# 15. COLLECTING EVIDENCE

HANGING up the phone, Sara had a look around Lenny's place. She was alone for the time being, because she hadn't phoned anyone else or reported it. This was going to remain off the books so to speak, until she figured out what in the hell was going on. Not just anyone could be trusted right now. Some twisted individual seemed to have it out for Lenny. First his co-worker, now his wife? This wasn't random by any means. This was personal. Thirty-some years on the police force with a treasure trove of scumbags socked away due to Lenny's police skills didn't exactly narrow down a potential list of suspects.

As Lieutenant Whitten walked around and inspected the doorjambs and windows, there were no signs of forced entry, as far as she could see. It was not at all completely out of the question for the doors to have been unlocked. The abduction did take place early in the day in a good neighborhood, she thought.

Poor Tessa. Sara hoped to God that she didn't end up like Leopold. If that were the case, she would have to turn her badge in along with Lenny. First off, because she could never arrest or fault the guy. Even if taking the law into your own hands wasn't exactly what being an officer of the law was about. Secondly, because she would help him pursue the bastard if it came to that.

Walking down the hallway, the click clack of Sara's stilettos on the ceramic tile floor was the only sound echoing in the air. With her hand on her pistol, she cleared every room left in the house, carefully stepping around the blood smear in the hallway. She would circle back around after the all clear to collect any evidence.

Going into the darkroom, there weren't really any signs of a struggle. She collected the Nikon camera and placed it into an evidence bag, as well as a roll of film that was lying on the metal table. She carefully started dusting the table as well as the door handle for prints. There were a couple, which she carefully lifted. Thank goodness that Tessa was a good housekeeper, otherwise she could have spent all night collecting fingerprints. Inspecting the few that were collected, her instincts told her that these prints had to be Tessa's. Much too small for a male. Besides, the intruder more than likely wore gloves, or was careful to wipe any prints he may have left. As far as she knew, nothing had been found on the vic,... or Katy rather, from this morning.

Moving out into the hallway, she swabbed the blood sample, and sealed the long wooden q-tip in a clear cylindrical collection tube. Hearing movement out toward the kitchen area, she unlatched her gun and quietly slipped off her shoes. Creeping down the dark hallway with her gun drawn, she thought if this were the perp returning to the scene of the crime, it was almost too easy. Easing around the corner, she spotted an elderly gentleman standing at the kitchen island with a butter knife in his hand, and a gun sitting on the kitchen island in front of him.

"Put the knife down, put your hands in the air, and back away from the counter" she commanded, as her pistol was trained on his heart.

With a gun pointed directly at his ticker, the butter knife dropped with a clatter as the man's eyes went saucer-like with confusion.

Shooting his hands straight up, he began babbling, "Please, don't shoot. Don't shoot. I just wanted a peanut butter and jelly sandwich, and I'm out of bread."

Sara narrowed her eyes, surveying the man. He had to be what, in his 80's?

"What's your name?"

"Ma ma ma Mr. Perkins. I I I I live ac c c c c cross the street. Tessa don't mind. She said. She told me anytime I n n need something I I I I can come over."

Keeping her finger on the trigger, and her eyes trained on the man, Sara slowly lowered her weapon. *The gun on the counter must be Lenny's piece.* She had heard Lenny and Tessa speak of the infamous Mr. Perkins. Poor guy. Had the onset of Dementia or Alzheimer's. Ironically, she couldn't remember which. They felt sorry for him, and always tried to help him out, but he did have a tendency to get confused and overstep his bounds in the neighborhood, oftentimes just letting himself in to other people's homes unannounced.

Surveying that he was not a threat, Sara holstered her pistol. "Mr. Perkins, I've heard Lenny talk about you. You live next door, right? I'm Lieutenant Sara Whitten, Lenny's boss. I think Lenny may have told you I was coming to talk to you?"

He nodded, all the while still keeping his hands in the air.

Sara pushed aside her blazer, to reveal the holstered pistol. "Mr. Perkins, I've put my gun away. You can lower your hands now."

Mr. Perkins slowly lowered his hands. "Can I make a peanut butter and jelly sandwich," he asked, like a kid in a candy store.

Sara nodded in approval and smiled. "Yes, you can make a peanut butter and jelly sandwich."

A jovial smile spread across his face. "Why thank you, Miss Sara."

"You're welcome. Mr. Perkins, did you see anything out of the ordinary today?"

"Well, Miss Sara, I already told Lenny that Miss Tessa had company this morning right after he left. Right around 7:30, I was on my porch swing drinking my morning coffee and reading the newspaper. Never any good news in the newspaper. A black sedan with four doors pulled out of his garage. Dark windows, though. Couldn't see who was in the car." Motioning to his wire rimmed glasses, he said, "the old eyesight ain't what it used to be."

Taking a bite of his sandwich, he swallowed slow and hard. Whispering like a child he said, "Is there… something wrong Miss Sara?"

Sara looked at him and decided he was just an old man, with not all of his marbles in play. "No, Mr. Perkins. Nothings wrong. You just go back on over to your house and stay there tonight. Lenny and Tessa are having um….an exterminator come, so you can't be in the house for awhile. You know, they …have ants." She hated lying to the old man, but as of right now, this was a top secret investigation, and she really didn't need the old man mucking up her crime scene, or worse, possibly running into the perp if he decided to come back for some reason.

With a surprised look on his face, he exclaimed, "Oh. Hard to get rid of those little buggers once they get in. I had ants once. Had to throw out all of my cereal, and all of my sugar."

"Okay, Mr. Perkins," Sara sighed. Approaching the island, she reached into her blazer, and pulled out one of her cards. Holding it out to him, he shuffled around the granite top, and took the card. With her hand lightly on his back, she walked him towards the front door.

"If you remember anything else about this morning, you give me a call, okay? Anytime, day or night."

Mr. Perkins shook his head. Just before crossing the threshold of the front door that Sara was holding open for him, Mr. Perkins spoke. "Oh, I almost forgot, Miss Sara." Reaching into his back pocket, he pulled out an envelope. "This must be for you. It was on the counter" As he held the envelope in his age spotted hands, he pointed to a smear of grape jelly. "I put it in my pocket, because I didn't want to make more of a mess of it," he blushed.

Sara looked at the envelope, which her name was scripted across. In the events of the evening, she completely forgot about the note to which Lenny referred to in his voicemail. Damn, it had been awhile since she had been out behind her desk and out in the field. Taking the envelope from his grip, she thanked Mr. Perkins and bid him a good night. She watched him cross the street before closing the door.

Walking back down the hallway, Sara grabbed her heels. She wasn't too anxious to put them back on.

Yes, they were sexy, and professional, but also about as comfortable as slamming your hand in a car door after wearing them all day, at least five days a week. She often thought that whoever decided that women should wear them should be shot. She was more of a jeans and t-shirt kind of girl when not in the office, except for special occasions, of course. Jeans and a t-shirt looked great with some flat soled knee high boots or some all star sneakers. As a matter of fact, home was going to be her next stop. Just long enough to change her clothes.

Walking back to the kitchen island, Sara stood there for a few moments, just staring at the pistol that was lying there. Gathering the nerve, she opened the envelope and read the note inside…

*Sara,*
*The body we found today at Seminole was no accident. The first note, I found on the body. The second note was left for me at home. He has Tessa. There is blood in the hallway, and I know for sure that he was in the darkroom, so make sure you dust for prints. I am going after him. I also need to know the identity of the Seminole vic as soon as you hear from the ME to see if we can narrow down a list of suspects-*
*Lenny*

She read the two mini notes that came with Lenny's handwritten note. The first stated that Lenny "couldn't save this one, but he would be given 24 hrs from that point to save the next." The second indicated that he had 17 hours left, to save Tessa.

*Shit*, she thought. Lenny needed to know the identity of the first vic, immediately. Taking out her phone, she saw the missed text message. Opening it, she saw it was from Lenny. A picture of a license plate. She immediately forwarded it to both Layne and Wilshire, with instructions to keep it hush, hush, and to meet her back at the office in thirty minutes. She dialed Lenny's number, and in doing so, decided that it was better to let him know over a voicemail, that the identity of the first vic was Leopold, rather than to keep it from him any longer, and possibly hinder his chances on saving Tessa. While waiting for an answer, Sara glanced once again at the gun sitting on the island. Holy Mother. Of.

Hell. Why didn't she recognize it sooner? She should know that gun anywhere. It was Lenny's police issued gun.

The ringing seemed to go on for an eternity before she finally got connected to his voicemail. Her message to him entailed Manny's positive id on this morning's vic, as well as her findings at his house.

In a desperate plea before ending the call, she said, "Lenny, please don't do anything stupid. I'm staring at your piece that you left on the kitchen island as I speak. I know what that means."

Hanging up the phone, Sara gathered the evidence she had collected, the notes, and Lenny's gun, and high tailed it out of there. Her first stop was going to be back at the precinct to the forensics department. No time right now to stop and change her clothes. She had already shot a text to Wilshire and Layne to meet her back at HQ. This was more than a one woman or one man job, and she trusted those two detectives with her life. And Lenny's. And Tessa's.

# 16. INTO THE UNKNOWN

BEFORE entering into the tree line, Lenny set the countdown timer on his watch to sixteen hours. From the time he left the crime scene at work this morning until now, had been roughly eight hours. He knew that realistically, he should call and wait for backup. Well, this wasn't exactly your typical realistic situation, now was it? Realistically, he didn't expect today to go at all like the events that had unfolded. Realistically, he expected to be wining and dining his wife right now. Realistically, he expected to be giving his wife the news of his retirement, and the vacation tickets to celebrate the start of their new chapter in life. Realistically, he was not going to waste any precious time. He was here right now, and was not going to wait for back up. Law enforcement or not, he didn't plan to let the rules dictate any of his movements. Not on this case. Besides, Sara or anyone else on the team would recognize his car on the side of the road.

They were detectives. They were smart enough to figure out where he went. If worse came to worse, they could always try to triangulate his position through the gps on his cell phone, of which he now switched the ringer and all alarm sounds to silent.

Lenny scanned the brush for bent grass, footprints, and other tell tale signs. He followed the disturbances, like a trail of breadcrumbs, to the outer edge of the dense brush. There was only set of very large male footprints, and they originated from the vehicle. Whomever was in that car hightailed it straight into the brush. It had been a while since he had had to track anyone, but it was like riding a bike. It all came rushing back to him, like he had never stopped.

He set down the duffle bag, and removed some camouflage fatigues, steel toed boots, and other necessities the situation called for. Stripping off all of his other clothing down to his boxers, he changed into his new uniform for this mission. Rolling up his other clothing, he packed it back into the duffle. Arming himself with a knife, and a few strategically placed guns, the last thing he armed himself with was an electronic bug repellent.

The sun was quickly starting to reach the Western horizon. The expansive thick canopy was blocking most of the daylight that was still left. It would be great during the day, to keep the hot sun at bay. At dusk though, it was going to make the daylight hours even shorter.

Lenny didn't much care for the earlier afternoon's shower making the air that much more thick with humidity, and even thicker with mosquitoes. Damn things should be the state bird. Fortunately, it was a typical Florida summer rain shower. Rained for twenty minutes around 4:00, then cleared up, like it was never there to begin with.

What he was thankful for though, was the fact that some moisture was able to permeate the ground. It left the soil soft and slightly muddy under the dry brush, making footprints easier to find, and much easier to track. He slung his duffle over his shoulder and briskly got moving South, into the unknown wilderness.

# 17. FORMING A PLAN

LIEUTENANT. Sara Whitten pulled her white Toyota Camry into her designated parking spot at the precinct. She burst through the glass doors past homicide, directly to the forensics department.

She carefully handed several sealed plastic baggies to Manny Sanchez. He immediately started to visually inspect the notes, blood sample, and print kits, through their plastic coverings. "Listen, Manny, I need these processed on the DL. And, I need it ASAP. It involves some of our own."

The quizzical and hurt look that spread over Manny's golden skinned face, prompted Sara to say, "I'm sorry, Manny. It's an ongoing investigation. I can't tell you anything at this point. If you want to help, then just please get this done for me, and let me know anything the moment you find it."

Manny Sanchez, head of the forensics department, shook his head in understanding. "I'm right on it Lieutenant." Splaying his hand out, onto his own chest, he said, "You can count on me, Sara."

Sara softly smiled at him, while fighting the urge to embrace him for some sort of comfort. "I know I can, Manny. Thank you."

Sara and Manny had a mutual attraction for each other, but it never went anywhere, other than office flirtation. It was not forbidden, but likely frowned upon by the department. It was much more than some stupid office crush though. Manny had it all. He was smart, quite the looker, and successful in his career. Honest, kind, caring, and a perfect gentleman. She could go on and on, but there was just something missing, although she couldn't put it in words. He was also ten years her junior, although she looked ten years younger than her actual age. She had dated men before, but none that would ever lead to anything serious. Maybe that is why she always found some excuse to not pursue things with Manny. He made it very clear to her in the past, that she was all he wanted, and that he would wait for her as long as he had to. She was afraid of true happiness. One too many times as a homicide detective, she had witnessed someone's heart being ripped right out of their chest, because of being in love, or loving someone. Hell, look at Lenny right now. His emotions were making him a weak and vulnerable target.

She watched as Manny walked into his lab and closed the door. They briefly made eye contact through the window of his lab room, before he pulled the blinds for privacy. *Snap the hell out of it Sara*, she thought to herself.

Turning around and walking into the homicide division, she approached the desks of Detectives Layne and Wilshire. Motioning them to follow her into her office, she kept walking until she reached her desk. Detective Layne acknowledged her, and held his finger up to signal that he would be right there, as he was on the phone, and Detective Wilshire was flipping through this mornings case file.

The two of them couldn't be a more opposite looking pair of partners. Detective Layne was tall and broad with a muscular build. He looked more like a tattoo artist/ biker/ rock star, with his long dark hair and chiseled features. The tattoos and gauged ears sealed the look. He had never changed his look when he transferred out of doing undercover drug operations, into the homicide division.

Detective Wilshire had a similar physique, but looked a little less intimidating. He was a little more cleaned up and polished around the edges. He had a bit of an edgy look to him, minus the gauged ears and long hair. Unlike Detective Layne in his jeans and form fitting Affliction shirts, Wilshire always dressed sharp, in designer clothing. Usually a suit, minus the tie and vest. His hair was always nothing less than perfect. He actually looked like he should be leaping off the pages of a magazine. A real ladies man. He was the kind of man you saw, and expected to see driving a Mercedes. Sara leaned very fast that you could not judge a book by its cover. Layne was a hard ass for sure, but he was also a big softie. He would be the first one to help an old lady cross the street,…or discretely beat the shit out of a guy that was a woman or a child abuser. Wilshire had a reputation as a playboy, but Sara saw through the charade, and deduced that it was probably due to his own fear of commitment, not dissimilar to hers. She was fond of both of them. They were both respectful to her, and did not tolerate any BS from anyone else on the force giving their Lieutenant guff, just because she was a female. They were very protective of her, and she knew without any doubt or hesitation, that she absolutely and unequivocally could trust them both with her life. In this line of work, that was a huge benefit of relief. She liked that about both of them. Plus, they were both really great Detectives.

Reaching her office, she settled behind her desk, as the two large and intimidating Officers entered the room. She signaled for both of the Detectives to close the door and have a seat. Without any question or hesitation, they each sat down in the two wing backed leather chairs that were set on the opposite side from which Lt. Whitten sat. She leaned forward in her chair, resting her tightly clasped hands on her dark wooden desk.

Looking between the both of them she said, "I have to fill you two in on some things. We are going to keep this between us. Anyone else will be filled in on a need to know basis. I have Manny doing some forensic work right now. If you have anything that needs to go to the lab, it goes to Manny only. Are we clear?"

"Crystal, Lieutenant," they both said in unison.

"Good," she said. Looking at Detective Layne, she asked, "Did you get anything off of that plate I sent you to run?"

"Yeah. The plate doesn't match the car. I had a black and white pull the VIN number off of the vehicle. It is registered to a woman named Nellie Hinkle. I pulled her driver's license." Detective Layne pulled a sheet of paper out of a manila folder and handed it across the desk to his Lieutenant. "Funny thing is, Lieutenant, the plate that is on the vehicle is registered to one of our cars here in the compound lot. Wilshire and I already went to speak to this Nellie Hinkle. We didn't get an answer, so we asked around the neighborhood. Seems she is a snowbird, and is back in New Jersey for the summer. She's not even here, so apparently the car was stolen right out of her garage."

"Shit!" exclaimed Sara. "So much for any leads off of that. Have either of you been able to get a contact number for this woman?"

Wilshire spoke up, "We're already on it,
Lieutenant. So far, all we have gotten is her
answering machine. We left a message. With any luck,
she will get back to us soon. We also explained the
situation to her local police, and they put out a BOLO.
If they find her, they are going to escort her back to her
home, and assist her in calling us back. They were
made aware that this is an urgent and time sensitive
case. As soon as we know anything, we'll let you
know."

Sara was relieved to hear that these two didn't need
micromanaging to do their jobs. They had done, and
were doing everything that she would have directed
them to do as their Lieutenant.

"Okay, then," she said. Sighing, and dreading the
inevitable, she proceeded to fill them both in on
everything that she had learned from Lenny over the
phone, and from being at his house, as well as the bad
news she heard from Manny, concerning the ID of this
morning's Jane Doe.

At the news of Kate Leopold's death, Layne's gut hit
rock bottom, and it took everything he had to make
sure that the burger and fries he ate for lunch didn't
make a splash onto the floor. A burning rage welled up
inside of him. Starting to shake, he wanted to hit
something. To throw something. Or someone. He sat
there with his eyes closed, rocking himself in the chair,
trying to gather himself and his thoughts. So. Not.
Happening. Standing up, he tossed the wingback chair
he had been sitting on.

"Fuuuuuuck! Fuck! I'm gonna wring that son of a
bitch's neck!"

Detective Wilshire signaled the Lieutenant with a
raise of his palm, to stay seated. Standing up himself,
he walked over to Layne, who was now with his back
to them, gazing out the glass windows through clouded
eyes. His arms were crossed around his trembling

body. Wilshire grasped his shoulders and spun him
around, resisting Layne's rejection, and pulled him in
close, to hold him tight.

Layne broke down in sobs. Through a broken voice,
Layne managed to heave out, "I loved her, man." His
voice grew almost inaudible, and he reiterated, "I
loved her."

"I know. I know," Wilshire reassured him, stroking
his back. "I know it hurts, buddy, but I need you need
to pull yourself together, so we can go find the piece of
shit that did this to her, okay?"

Layne took a deep sigh, and stepped back from the
embrace. Wiping his tears, and getting his breath under
control, he turned to his Lieutenant. "I'm really sorry,
Lieutenant. I'm sorry," he said, waving his hands in
the air.

Lieutenant Sara Whitten stood from her chair, and
walked around her desk to pick up the tipped over
wingback. She set the chair in it's upright position, and
casually strolled over to Layne. Looking deep into his
eyes, she grabbed a hold of him, and pulled him in
quick, where she held him in a tight embrace. "I
understand, Layne. She was one of our own," she
whispered in his ear, with one arm embracing his
strong back, and the other holding the nape of his neck.

Holding Layne's resting head on her shoulder, Sara
took as much comfort from it, as she was giving.
Reaching out, she took Detective Wilshire's hand. The
three of them stood there in a moment of silence,
before returning to their seats.

"Learning what we now know about the plate, this
could possibly be an inside job. I don't want to believe
that, but it's looking like that could be a definite
possibility" Sara said. "So far we have Detective
Leopold being brutally assaulted and murdered,
Detective Shane being toyed with, along with his wife
being abducted by the same maniac that got to Kate,
and now we know the plate on the vehicle was stolen

out of our compound lot. It isn't making much sense right now, but it's what we have to go on."

Detectives Layne and Wilshire looked at each other and nodded. Detective Layne responded, "Yeah, Lieutenant. We're definitely onto that vibe now that we've found out that the Jane Doe this morning was actually Katy. I mean, Detective Leopold. Add that to the information we found out about the license plate, plus the personal target directed towards Detective Shane? Seems too much of a coincidence. We need to make sure we keep it on the DL. Anyone could be involved."

Discussing the facts of the case, Lieutenant Whitten, nor her team of Detectives ruled Verde completely out, because he had not been apprehended yet. No one knew where he was. It wasn't impossible, but highly improbable that he was their man. The why escaped her. For the life of her she couldn't figure it out. Lenny was a stand up guy. Why anyone would have anything against him she just couldn't fathom. Especially if it were an inside job. He was a great detective, a great mentor to the rookie detectives. Not one person on the force had a beef with him as far as she knew. On top of that, he was getting ready to retire. He hadn't put in his official notice yet, but Sara could tell it was coming.

"Alright, then," Sara said. "Let's keep everything we find out between us, Manny, Lenny, and Detective Thorne. Detective Thorne phoned me earlier. Apparently he was headed to Miami for the weekend with a lady friend when he received voicemails from both myself and Lenny. He said he was on the Alley, about to go right by the area, and that he would check it out. I haven't heard from him since, but we are all aware that cell reception out there isn't easy to get"

Layne and Wilshire looked at each other and didn't need to speak words to know what the other was thinking. There was no way in fuck that either one of them would be putting Thorne in the loop of anything,

unless it was a hangman's noose. If they found out it
was him behind all of this, that is.

With all of the colleagues in agreement, they decided
the only other lead they could follow at the moment,
would be to just head out to the Alley, and see where it
would lead them. She shot Lenny a text message,
filling him in with the information on the VIN number
and the stolen license plate, along with the fact that
she, Layne, and Wilshire, and Thorne were all coming,
hoping he would get it. She didn't know exactly where
he was right now, but if he were out in the thick of the
Everglades, she could only keep her fingers crossed,
that he could get a cell signal.

# 18. BREADCRUMBS

LENNY covered a lot of ground quickly. He checked his cell phone periodically to see if Lieutenant Whitten had gotten back to him regarding the license plate on the black Lincoln.

He read the text, which made him even more confused. All the while, he was thinking this was the work of someone he had put away...but an inside job? Didn't make sense. Why? Why would someone do this? These are the things he intended to find out. Or not. When he found whomever it was that did this to Katy and Tessa, it was no holds barred. Answers or not.

Even with all the perplexity, he felt a wave of relief come over him, to see that Whitten, Layne, Wilshire, and Thorne all had his back. At least if something did happen to him out here, Tessa could still be rescued by one of them.

By now, it was dark out, and the full cover of the trees made it even darker. Looking at the countdown on his watch, he estimated it was nearly 10:00 pm. The countdown was at eleven hours and winding down. Placing his cell phone back in his shirt pocket, he unsheathed his flashlight. He was exhausted, but he could sleep later. He was going to go, and he was going to track, until he absolutely could not physically keep his body upright, or his eyes open.

Hearing some movement up ahead, Lenny shined his flashlight in the general direction. He could see the brush moving, but did not see the culprit of the movement. There was no wind to speak of tonight, so something or someone disturbed it. He would have to be extra vigilant in this neck of the woods. Not only was there a delusional madman out here, but dangerous animals. Ones that liked to hunt prey, particularly at night.

Picking up his pace, he had his flashlight in his left hand, and his gun in the other. Looking straight ahead, he walked toward where the disturbance had been. Scanning the flashlight over the area, he saw nothing. He wasn't sure if he thought that was a good sign, or a bad sign. Probably just a deer, he thought. Possibly an armadillo, raccoon, squirrel or opossum.

Turning off his light for a moment, he stopped to listen. He didn't hear anything out of the ordinary. He closed his eyes, and let his senses do their work. Smoke. He smelled smoke. Clicking the light back on, he continued on, moving the brush out of the way, so he could get into a small clearing. Off in the distance, he saw some glowing embers. Remnants of a recent campfire. This, he thought was a good sign. No one in their right damn mind would be out here camping in the middle of nowhere. No one in their right damn mind. This meant that he was definitely on the right path. He wasn't sure how much of a head start they had gotten on him, but he knew he was getting close

Coming out of the brush, something across his torso stopped his momentum. At first he thought it must be a vine, until he shined his light onto it. It appeared to be a clear filament, like fishing line. He reached into his pocket, and cut the filament with a quick slice of his knife. Hearing a swooping sound, Lenny abruptly reacted and felt a rush of air blow by his face, as a slender bamboo branch came dangerously close to whacking him, right in the throat area. Taking a moment to get his composure, he realized that this was not some sort of animal trap, or a coincidental happening, but an intentional set up. He would have to be much more careful, to not underestimate his opponent. If not for his lightning fast reflexes, due in large part to his martial arts training, a direct hit to the throat could have left him gasping for air. Possibly crushed his windpipe, depending on speed, weight, and trajectory of the branch. He was fortunate in that aspect, but the branch did catch him on his right upper arm, leaving a pretty good gash. Lenny figured out exactly what was going on. The trail thus far was easy to follow. So easy in fact, that he knew the abductor wanted to be followed by him, just not too closely.

Emerging from the brush into the clearing, Lenny turned his flashlight off. Once reaching the campfire, he listened for a moment for any footfalls. Upon hearing nothing, he turned the flashlight on and scanned the area. Against a large tree, he found a length of rope that had been tied around the tree, with just enough excess to fit a 120 lb woman snugly against it. He immediately recognized it as the same type of rope he found in the Lincoln Continental. Looking more closely at the ground, he saw two sets of prints. One very small, and one very large. He was relieved at the fact that Tessa was still walking. Running rather, at closer inspection of the length of

stride. It appeared as though her captor wasn't
holding her close, or walking behind her, but rather
beside her. He knew for sure these were Tessa's prints.
He could feel it in his gut. Small, size five confirmed
by the imprint of the shoe, with a number five
contained within a circle. Tessa's size. He knew from
shoe shopping with Tessa, that not many women wore
size fives, making them a pain in the ass to find.
Average women's shoe size was a seven.

   Lenny decided to take the hint, and fall back a little.
He could make up the time later, and could move
quicker if he were to get a little rest. He sat in the very
spot against the tree, where Tessa had recently been.

   The lunatic he was tracking was indeed extremely
dangerous, but the elements could kill you, or slow you
down just as well. Unzipping the duffle bag, he
removed a bottled water, and a pack of peanut butter
crackers. He gathered the length of rope from around
the tree, and stuffed it into the duffle. Either to use for
evidence, or maybe he would use it to strangle the guy,
in which case it would still be evidence. Lenny quietly
chuckled, and smirked at the thought.

   It was a hot and sticky night. Even after the sun went
down, it was near eighty degrees, and the humidity was
even higher. It was important to keep hydrated, to
lessen muscle cramping and fatigue. He didn't have
any idea how far this hike would take him. So far, he
estimated that he had gone about four to five miles. His
leg and back muscles ached because of the intense
walking, stooping, and squats that tracking required,
which he had been doing over the past five hours.
Noticing that part of his jacket was blood soaked, he
figured he needed to take a look at the damage done by
the bamboo branch. Gingerly he peeled it off of his
right shoulder and arm. A wince settled upon his face,
and a "mother fucker," softly escaped his lips. He
removed a t-shirt from his duffle and moistened it with
a bit of water to clean the wound. It definitely wasn't

pretty. A large and deep gash continued to pulse blood down his arm. It definitely required stitches. There was only one thing for him to do. Getting up on his knees, he angled himself down, with his arm towards the smoldering remnants of the campfire. Readying himself, he took three quick and successive breaths, and he pushed his arm into the searing hot embers. Inside, he screamed in agony as the sizzle of burning flesh filled the air. Sitting back up, his hands trembled, spilling some of the water bottle's contents onto the ground. In between his trembles, he managed to get some of the water splashed onto the blackened wound, and lightly pat it dry with his blood soaked t-shirt. Digging through his duffle, he opted for some sunburn spray with Novocain, to numb it up some. He was in such great pain, that he didn't even feel the sting of the spray. With his ass planted firmly on the ground, he leaned his head back against the tree. Closing his eyes, he raised the bottle to his parted lips, and the water soothed his parched mouth and throat. In the dim moonlight, he alternated sipping the water, and eating the crackers. It was no Ruth's Chris filet mignon, but it was going to have to do.

As his body took in the nourishment, the heat, exhaustion, and pain overwhelmed him. With all of the adrenaline pumping through his veins, it didn't register before he sat back against the tree. It came surging over his body like a tidal wave. He couldn't fight it. His eyelids grew heavy, as his body demanded to rest. In his mind, he was fighting to stay awake, but it was a futile battle. Glancing down at the solar green glow of his watch timer indicated that there was 10 hours left. Okay, maybe just a twenty minute cat nap, he narrowly convinced himself. His breathing slowed, and his eyelids drew to a close.

# 19. MAKING ROOM

SHE was moving much to slow for his taste, so
Thorne wrapped his hand around Tessa's upper arm,
and pulled her along. "Tessa, I know you're tired, but
we have to keep moving," he urged, with impatience.

With a crossed look settling on her face, Tessa shook
his hand off of her arm. She stopped and placed her
hands on her hips. "Where the hell are we going,
Bobby? I mean, shouldn't we have been back to the
road by now? I know I was out of it for a bit, and I
don't remember getting here after the car accident, but
I couldn't have been out for *that* long." Now starting to
whine, she said, "I just want to get out of this
nightmare and go home. Where is your partner?
Where's my husband? Where is Lenny," she
demanded to know. She had been manhandled one too
many times today, and she was just about over the

shit.

Turning on the charm, and pulling her in close for a reassuring hug, Detective Thorne lifted her face and looked directly into her eyes. "I know you're scared and tired, Tessa. We're not going back to the road where your car accident was, because that is not where my car is." Nodding off in the distance, he said, "I actually have a cabin not too far from here. That is where we are going. I don't know where Lenny is, but I'm sure he's looking for you. I just need you to be strong for a little while longer, okay?"

Tessa swallowed the lump that was forming in her throat, but that did not stop a warm stream escaping the corners of her eyes. His smell was familiar, and...*wait a minute. How did he know about the car accident, if his car was not parked on the highway, unless...*It made her want to immediately pull away from him. Fighting against her body's instincts, she didn't give away any hints of her revelation. *Impossible. What the hell was wrong with her? There had to be another explanation. He was the only one here trying to get her out of this mess, and away from the damn masked lunatic.*

"Okay," she said, with her lips starting to quiver. Wiping her eyes and getting her composure, she said with confidence, "Let's do this. Let's go." Stopping abruptly after taking just a few steps, she turned to him and said, "Oh, and Bobby, thank you, and... how much longer do you think it will be? I could really use some aspirin," she said as she lightly touched the side of her head that now was black and blue with a nicely formed goose egg .

"Tessa, I don't know exactly how much longer it will be, but very soon, this will all be over." Eagerly taking advantage of their brief pause, he removed two bottled waters and a bag of pretzels for them to share. "Here, I don't have any aspirin, but this will make you feel better," he said, handing her the items. At a very

minimum, it would keep her mouth occupied for a
while, so she couldn't ask him what time it was. Again.
"Let's move," he said with authority.

They hiked through the wilderness for several more
hours. Tessa was on the verge of calling it quits. She
was exhausted, and just wanted to rest. She didn't care
anymore. She could lie down right there and fall asleep
within minutes, considering it was close to three
o'clock in the morning the last time she asked Bobby
what time it was. She felt like a kid on a road trip,
constantly asking what time it was, just to find out that
only fifteen minutes had passed since the last time she
asked. He was probably getting annoyed with it by
now, but she didn't care. She was annoyed too, with
this entire day, and everything about it. Just when she
was about to give up for the night, a small wooden
cabin came into view. It reminded her somewhat, of a
Thomas Kincaid painting. She wanted to burst out into
a full sprint, but her legs were currently as stable as
jell-o. Butterflies of excitement started swirling around
in her stomach at the thought of finally being able to
rest, and possibly getting a bite of something real to
eat. On second thought, a hot shower to wash away the
filth, along with all of her aches and pains would be
even better. She could not get to that cabin fast
enough. It was calling to her like a moth to a flame.

Detective Thorne squashed her spirits, when he
turned to her, placed his hand against her chest and
said, "Tessa, I want you to stay right here. I have to do
a sweep of the cabin to make sure it's all clear. We've
been fortunate enough to not run into the guy that did
this to you. It's a safety precaution. You understand?
You stay right here, up against this tree, until I come
and get you. If you hear anyone, or see any shadows, I
want you to hide, okay?"

As he was backing her up against the tree, she was
looking at him, looking at her, while patiently awaiting
a response. She took a deep breath that exuded disgust.

"Alright, okay. Just hurry it up will you? I am so done with this whole day already."

Tessa settled in against the tree with her arms crossed, and watched Detective Thorne make his way to the cabin. By the time he got there, he was nothing but a small shadow off in the distance.

Detective Thorne walked the perimeter of the cabin, peering inside the windows. The snowy television sufficiently lit the small one room cabin enough for him to see that there was a man inside, who was snoring away on a plaid worn out sofa. Approaching the back door, he grasped the door handle, and the door cracked open. He snuck across the room, and withdrew his pistol, pointing it directly at the poor unsuspecting sleeper. He nudged the Larry the Cable Guy look a like with his foot. Completely startled, his eyes flew open, followed by him holding both hands in the air. Apparently, he noticed the Detective shield.

"I haven't done anything, Officer, Sir. What ever it is, I didn't do it. I was out fishin' all day. Got me some fresh snapper in the freezer if ya don't believe me," he stammered in a good ole boy Southern drawl.

"What's your name," Detective Thorn inquired.

"Sonny Holden. My name's Sonny Holden," the man answered, as if this would clear everything right up.

"Get up, Sonny, nice and slow, and take me to your boat," Detective Thorne ordered.

"Yeah, okay. Whatever you want. What's this about," he asked.

Getting no answer from Detective Thorne, Sonny sat up, and he wiped the sleep out of his eyes. He turned and started walking towards the back door. Detective Thorne was right behind him, with the muzzle of his gun in the small of Sonny's back.

"Nice and slow, and don't try anything stupid," Detective Thorne stated, as they were exiting the cabin.

Once outside, they walked across a small concrete

patio, then across some brick pavers, which led down
to an unlit dock. The dock was weather worn and old,
just like the cabin. Shabby is the word that came to
Thorne's mind. Some of the planks were warped,
causing them to be very uneven. Tripping or stubbing
your toes would be a definite probability, if you didn't
watch your step. There was a foul smell coming off of
the dock, reeking of rotting fish blood and guts, that
had been cooking in the hot Florida sun. Incidentally,
which made the rate of decay accelerate. The smell
was so horrid that Thorne had to stifle his gag reflex.
When he had been out here numerous times before, the
cabin had been unoccupied. Poor guy. Wrong place,
wrong time. Thorne needed his cabin, and so, he
needed to get rid of him. The fact that the guy had a
boat, was an added bonus. It would make his escape
even easier.

Reaching the end of the dock, Sonny turned around
and unclipped the set of keys from his belt. He handed
the boat keys to Detective Thorne. Thorne took them,
and shoved them into his pocket.

"Turn back around, and get on your knees with your
hands behind your back," he demanded.

Sonny barely got out a "why," when Detective
Thorne kicked the back of his knees causing them to
buckle.

"Do it," Thorne said with an even intensity.

Sonny might not be so willing to comply, had he
noticed Thorne stoop during their stroll on the dock, to
pick up a gutting knife that had been left lying there.

Sonny's knees hit the dock with a thud, and he placed
his arms behind his back. Scared and confused out of
his wits, he started pleading. "Please, Officer. What am
I being arrested for," he asked in bewilderment.

Detective Thorne placed his palm on top of the man's
head. "Your not," he muttered. His palm closed,
gathering a fistful of Sonny's shaggy mop. Yanking his
head back in a quick and fluid motion, Thorne deeply

raked the gutting knife across the Sonny's neck from his left ear to his right.

Not wanting to "get dirty," Thorne swiftly kicked the limp body off of the dock. A heavy splash broke the calm surface, as Sonny Holden sank into the murky water. Dropping the knife, it clamored at his feet, as Thorne watched the body disappear beneath the red pool. Satisfied, he turned on his heel, heading back towards the wooded perimeter where he had left Tessa.

## 20. HELP IS ON THE WAY

LIEUTENANT Whitten, and Detectives Layne and Wilshire pulled aerial and topography maps of the Everglades, deciding that it would be a good idea to first view and study the area. Maybe something would leap off of the pages at them.

With a red marker, Detective Layne placed a circle on the map, where the black Lincoln Continental was found. He leaned in, to take a closer look. "Here. Look," he said, running his finger down Route 29. "I'll bet money, this is where he was headed," shaking his head in approval. "Yeah. Down near Everglades City," he said, while tapping the map with his index finger. "It's isolated. Some areas are pretty remote and off the grid. Of course, there's also access to the water, in pretty much every direction, except to the North. Odds

are, he's heading South to Southwest. Ten Thousand
Islands is right off the coast." He looked up at Whitten
and Wilshire, who were both following what he said.
Detective Layne spoke up again and said, "We need to
cut this asshole off before he gets to the water.
Once he gets there, he could go anywhere. We could
never find him. Or her," he said with a grim undertone.
Lt. Whitten turned to Detective Wilshire. "You have
a four wheeler don't you? We'll be able to cover
ground more quickly that way, than on foot."
"Yeah. I can run back to the house and hook the
trailer up. I can be back here in about an hour," he said
while grabbing his keys out of his pocket.
Lt. Whitten thought about it for a minute and said,
"Why don't you two pick me up at my house? You
know where it is, and it's on the way. I need to run
home and change clothes. I don't think stilettos are
conducive to running around out in the Everglades,"
she said as she showed off her pumps.
"Actually, Lieutenant," Detective Layne spoke up, "if
it's cleared by you, I would like to split off from you
two, and come in from the other side by boat. That
way, we'll get more coverage. Maybe we can pinch
him in the middle?"
"Yes, Layne, great idea! That is fine by me. I didn't
know you had a boat," she said questioningly.
Detective Layne had a devilish grin spread across his
face. "Well, technically, I don't, but there is a whole
lot of them out in the compound?"
"I didn't hear that, Detective Layne, because you
didn't just say that," she said while covering her ears.
Then she winked at him.
"Lieutenant Whitten," Manny Sanchez called while
waiting at the door of the room.
Whitten, Layne, and Wilshire turned around.
Lieutenant Whitten motioned him to come in. "Yes,
Manny?"
"I got the results of the tests you brought in this

morning. All of them are pretty much inconclusive. No prints, no blood matches in the data base. I'm sorry Lieutenant," he said while looking down at the floor.

She touched him lightly on the arm and took the results file. "It's okay, Manny. You can only process the evidence that was collected and given to you. It's not your fault that the perp was careful not to leave us anything."

"I know. I just wish I could have been more of a help to the investigation."

"Thank you, Manny. If there is anything else we need, we will let you know," she said as she dismissed him from the room.

"Yes, Lieutenant," he said as he turned to walk out of the room.

"When are you going to stop tormenting that man," Detective Wilshire asked of his Lieutenant.

"What'" she giggled nervously. She didn't realize it was that obvious.

Both Layne and Wilshire rolled their eyes and said, "Nothing, Lieutenant."

Lieutenant Whitten walked over to the copy machine, made a copy of the maps, and handed them to Detective Layne. "Be careful. We'll see you out there," she said.

"You be careful," he cajoled.

As Lieutenant Whitten and Detective Wilshire were walking out of the homicide division, Detective Layne called to his partner. "Hey, Wilshire." Wilshire spun around, and Detective Layne gave him a nod and a thumbs up. Their own special understood version of a hug, or a fist or chest bump, or an "I love you man, be careful." Detective Wilshire understood exactly what his partner was trying to convey. He returned the nod and the gesture.

Once outside, Detective Wilshire said, as he was standing at the foot of his blue Mercedes, "Okay, Lieutenant, I'll be at your house to pick you up in about an hour."

"I'll be waiting." She ducked into the driver's seat of her white Toyota Camry, and pulled out of the precinct.

While they both headed in their separate directions, Detective Layne went out to the compound lot. He decided on a 2013 model, Everglades 295 CC twenty-nine foot center console with two 225hp Honda four stroke outboard motors. He hooked it up to his Ford F150, and set out heading South to the Marco Island boat launch. He chose Marco Island over Port of the Isles or Goodland, so he could scout the shores all the way from Marco to Everglades City.

# 21. MISHAPS

LENNY'S chocolate hued eyes flew open. His enlarged pupils darted around in the darkness. Momentarily he was in a fit of panic, because he actually did fall asleep. The sweat on his brow wasn't only due to the eighty degree temperature and high humidity. He hadn't been counting sheep in his dreams. Vivid, ghastly, and unthinkable images, reserved only for his nightmares, had flashed through his brain during his short unconsciousness. Outcomes of this entire fucked up situation, that he didn't even want to think about while he was awake. Reaching hastily over to his left trembling wrist, he looked at his timer. A sigh of relief expelled out of his lungs, when it registered that he had only been out for thirty minutes. A short thirty minute nap that did wonders.

Initially upon waking, emotionally, he was near drained. Physically, he felt as though he had slept for hours.

His leg muscles no longer burned, and the Novocain was doing its work on his arm. Standing up, he dusted himself off, and did a full body stretch. Popping yet another piece of Wrigley's gum, he discarded the wrapper on the ground, although he normally did not condone littering. In this instance, it would be a good and inconspicuous marker to let his colleagues know he was there, and that they were going in the right direction. He chewed the stuff so much, he had often wondered why he hadn't bought any stock in the large company yet. Picking up his duffle, he slung it over his back, and continued heading South.

In the darkness, it was not easy to track, but time was of the essence. He couldn't just sit there and wait for daybreak. By then, Tessa would be out of time. He opted to keep the flashlight turned off for the most part, because as much as he wanted to locate their position, he didn't want to give away his. Hell, for all he knew, the lunatic could be lying in wait for him. The stealthy quiet approach was better. Moving slow and methodically, periodically he would shine the light on the ground to pick up signs of which direction they were moving. Thus far, they had continued on foot, heading South. Lenny made a slightly educated guess, in knowing where they had entered from the road, combined with the direction they continued to move in, that they were headed at or around Everglades City, towards the water. One thing was for certain, and that was that they were quickly running out of land, unless they turned due East and headed towards Miami. That was a highly unlikely route, due to the distance to reach that destination on foot.

#

Wilshire arrived at his Lieutenant's modest two story split level. Lightly tapping his horn, he waited patiently in her driveway.

Whitten emerged from her door, and lightly jogged towards the BMW. *Holy shit.* He reached down and rearranged his manhood, because it was hard on sight. He had never seen her in civilian type clothes before. Her in tight fitting jeans, a clingy t-shirt, and a pair of black leather knee high boots. This was not good. Hopefully it was dark enough out for her not to notice the bulge in his pants, or his eyes popping out of his head. Or the tongue wagging.

"Let's go," she said, as she quickly entered, and settled into the passenger's seat, strapping herself in.

Wilshire didn't utter a word, because he was afraid he would sound like a fumbling for words kind of idiot, as they headed out of the gated community.

Detective Wilshire and Lt. Whitten pulled over and slowed to a stop when they saw Lenny's Mustang sitting on the side of the road. It was also very clear where the Continental had veered off the road, where the guardrail was a twisted and broken hunk of metal.

By this time, Coastal Towing was getting the black Lincoln Continental rigged up to be towed back to the department to be thoroughly swept and processed for evidence. Lt. Whitten instructed the tow truck driver to also tow the Mustang back to the station. She knew it was one of Lenny's sentimental prized positions, and she didn't want to leave it sit on the Alley, so some car thief could steal it and take off to Miami or somewhere else.

Detective Wilshire set up the ramps, and eased the four wheeler off of its trailer. Once completely off the trailer, he handed his Lieutenant a black full faced helmet, that matched his. She pulled her long flowing red locks back into a pony, and slipped the black cranium protector over her head. Turning to his Lieutenant, he tapped the back of the seat directly behind him, indicating for her to climb aboard. Thank God she wasn't driving, or she would have a lance poking into her back the whole time. Lieutenant Whitten hesitantly straddled her legs around the machine behind Detective Wilshire. Her hesitation had nothing to do with him at all, as she trusted him completely. It had everything to do with the fact that she had a fear of riding on anything that did not have a completely enclosed capsule. This would include four wheelers, motorcycles, dirt bikes, and any other similar moving vehicle, except convertible cars. She could do convertible cars, and even did those with a smile on her face, while the wind whipped through her hair.

Detective Whitten was aware of his Lieutenant's irrational fear, so he gingerly eased the throttle. He would try to break her in slowly, but they had a lot of time to make up. This was no time for dilly dallying around.

Lt. Whitten gritted her teeth, as the four wheeler set into motion. Hanging onto the cargo racks behind her was not doing much in the way of making her feel secure, as she bustled and bounced around like a rag doll.

Detective Whitten yelled over the loud motor, "You might want to hang onto me. Once we get across the open field and into the forest, it's going to get a whole lot bumpier."

Lt. Whitten released her death grip from the cargo racks, one hand at a time. From there, she hooked her thumbs around Detective Wilshire's belt loops. Her hands acting like a c-clamp.

Detective Wilshire's smile was concealed by the blacked out acrylic on his helmet. One by one, he pried his Lieutenant's hands from his belt loops, and pulled her arms tightly around his torso. She was his superior, and he completely respected that, and her. He was also a man, and that came with the instinct to be in control, and to lead and protect females.

This particular female, he would do anything for; although, he never let on the true intimacy of his feelings for her. She was enamored with Manny Sanchez, and he loved her too much to put her through all of the emotions. She was confused enough as it was, and needed to figure out if she and Manny were going to hook up or not. He had plenty of distractions to keep him busy during the meantime. That's all they were and would ever be though. Just distractions. His heart belonged to one. Driving with one hand, he held her hands there, with his. She leaned into his back, and held on for dear life, as he opened the throttle up, and they jetted off through the tree strew, and bumpy terrain.

The rhythmic vibration of the motor shook through her body. After about five minutes, she started to ease up a little. Riding the machine wasn't as terrifying as she had first imagined. What she could do without, was all of the dust and debris that was pelting her. She was glad that Detective Wilshire had full face helmets. At the very least, her eyes and mouth were protected. How miserable would this have been without them, with dirt and bugs flying into them? She shuddered at the thought.

Nearly an hour into their battering ride, they came across a recent camp fire. Pulling up along side it, they came to a stop. As Whitten dismounted from the four wheeler and stood, she rubbed her sore ass cheeks briskly with both hands, even before removing her helmet.

Catching her in the act, Detective Wilshire said with a chuckle, "Would you like some help with that, Lieutenant?" *Oh, shit. Did I just say that out loud?*

Without skipping a beat, she continued rubbing out the soreness of her battered glutes and said jovially, "Thanks for the offer, Detective, but I think I can handle it."

"Alright," he said. "Just don't say I never offered to do anything for you," as he removed her helmet for her, and handed her a flashlight.

"Let's take a look around here, but let's not get out of each other's line of sight," he said.

"Sounds good," she replied, while they simultaneously clicked their flashlights on.

Indicating the area around the campfire and four wheeler, Detective Wilshire said, "Why don't you start around this area, and I'll start at the perimeter." He shined his flashlight to the edge of the clearing. " I'll work my way in, and you can work your way out."

Lt. Whitten nodded in agreement, and immediately started looking for footprints, blood, or anything else that might give them some insight.

Detective Wilshire walked to the outer edge of the clearing, making sure to scan the ground on his way out.

Whitten immediately found evidence of three distinct different shoe prints. Judging by the size, she would say they belonged to two males and one small female. Knowing Lenny wore a size ten, she would bet money that the combat boot tread belonged to him. By process of elimination, obviously the smaller female print would belong to Tessa. She didn't know what size shoe she wore for sure, but she was petite. This left the last imprint. The largest imprint.

"Wilshire," she called out.

"Yeah," he replied.

"I found some prints over here. You find anything yet," she called out.

Not getting an immediate answer, Lt. Whitten shined her flashlight towards where Detective Wilshire had made his way to. He was North of her, back over where they came into the clearing from.

Shining his light into some brush, and leaning in for a closer inspection, Detective Wilshire yelled back.

"Lieutenant! I found some pretty fresh blood evidence over here."

Lt. Whitten started jogging towards Detective Wilshire with a pit in her stomach. At her arrival, Detective Wilshire pointed out the bamboo branch that had traces of blood, camouflage material, and skin on it. It wasn't enough to be alarming, so her tension eased. Taking a deep slow breath, her hammering heart returned to it's normal pace.

"Looks as though we're heading in the right direction. Let's continue heading South," she said.

"Definitely. I think Layne is right about heading towards Everglades City. It's only about five more miles due South of here," Detective Wilshire said.

They both headed back towards the four wheeler. This time, Lt. Whitten had no fears or qualms about mounting the off road beast.

Detective Wilshire was ready to put his helmet back on, and Lt. Whitten was about to do the same when she noticed something reflective directly behind the four wheelers driver's side rear tire. Shining her flashlight and squatting down, she picked up a wadded Wrigley's gum wrapper.

Holding it out in her palm, for Wilshire to see it, she said, "Detective?"

Without saying any more words to each other, they mutually knew that Detective Shane had definitely been here.

Whitten stuffed the wadded gum wrapper in the pocket of her form fitting Lucky jeans.

She and Detective Wilshire placed their helmets back on, and re- mounted the four wheeler. As Detective Wilshire eased the throttle, and the heavy four wheeler propelled forward, with the sound of crunching debris coming from beneath it's tires.

With her arms wrapped much more loosely around Detective Wilshire's waist, Lt. Whitten was getting used to the bumpy ride, and much to her surprise, was

actually starting to grow fond of it. It was actually
kind of exhilarating, she thought.

Detective Wilshire felt his Lieutenant's comfort level
rise, with her loosening grip. Knowing she was feeling
more comfortable, he continued easing the throttle
back, causing them to pick up speed, while continuing
to head South.

Suddenly, the four wheeler jarred to the right, as it's
driver's side front tire slammed into a huge pit in the
ground, that had been cleverly concealed with pine
needles, sticks, palm fronds, and other various kinds of
vegetative debris. Wilshire's throttle hand was jutted
forward, as his opposite hand came back towards him,
moving the steering column from a horizontal plane to
and almost vertical plane. He felt his elbow impact
Whitten in the side. Wilshire and Lt. Whitten were
both thrown violently forward, as the four wheeler lost
it's equal footing. The air came rushing so fast out of
Wilshire's lungs, as his abdomen impacted the left side
of the steering column. The punching pain radiated
through his gut, as he struggled to regain his breath. Lt.
Whitten was launched from behind Wilshire, doing a
quarter roll, mid air. Her right shoulder felt like it had
been struck by a base ball bat, when it impacted the
ground. Making a moaning sound, she rolled over onto
her back, removed her helmet, and grabbed her right
shoulder with her left hand. Sitting up, she started
moving her shoulder socket in a circular motion. She
felt no pain. It was just going to leave a good bruise,
with a couple weeks worth of soreness.

After regaining his breath, Detective Wilshire
removed his helmet, and dismounted the four wheeler,
whose back tires were no longer touching the ground.
Rushing over to Whitten, he kneeled down beside her
and placed his palm on the middle of her back.
"Lieutenant, are you okay," he asked with trepidation.
He didn't know if he could live with himself if he hurt
her.

Still cupping her right shoulder, she said, "My shoulder is a little banged up, but I'll live."

Detective Wilshire didn't say a word, but was searching her eyes for forgiveness.

"It's okay, Wilshire," she said. Using her left hand, she grabbed his right and gave it a squeeze. "This was not your fault. It was an accident. I don't hold you responsible in any way. Now, help me get up off of my ass," she joked, as she kept her right arm folded in close to her body, and extended her left arm out for a helping hand.

Positioning himself in front of his Lieutenant, Whitten placed his feet just over the tops of hers. With her legs bent, and their opposite arms engaged, he gave a slight pull. Whitten popped up off the ground, right into his embrace. He held her firmly within his arms for a few moments. Closing his eyes, he leaned his face down into her hair and took a deep breath of her lavender scented auburn locks.

Being entombed within his cocoon didn't feel at all awkward. Whitten felt a warm wash of a feeling spread through her, that she had never felt before. It actually felt…right. It felt safe.

"Can you stand by yourself okay," he asked. Uncasing his arms from around her, he slid his hands from her back, down over her sides and settled them onto her outer hips, to steady her buckling knees.

Locking her knees into place, and getting steady on her feet, Lieutenant Whitten shook off the brief moment of unstableness. "Yeah, Wilshire," she said. Taking a step back away from him, she continued, "Thanks. I'm good now."

She wasn't sure what made that feeling wash over her, and buckle her knees. Was it a result of being shook up from the accident, or was it the intense attraction to Wilshire that just slammed into her like a ton of bricks?

She didn't know if Wilshire felt it too, or if it was one

sided, but she didn't want the moment to grow awkward. Glancing around Wilshire at the immobile four wheeler, and seeing that it was not going to be taking them any further, she said, "I guess we have no choice but to pound the ground now."

Detective Wilshire felt the palpable tension between them and responded in agreement. "Let's move out, soldier," he wittily replied. He had to fight the urge to give her a light slap on her superbly round rump, as she turned and walked a couple of steps ahead of him. Her perfect blend of femininity and toughness was extremely appealing. Her exterior was just gorgeous, but her personality was just like "one of the guys."

Lost in his brief trance, she stopped and turned to him. "You coming or what," she asked.

"Yeah, sorry," he said through his lust filled fog. Detective Wilshire quickly closed the short distance in between them. They continued trudging onward in perfect synchronicity.

## 22. SET UP

TESSA recognized Thorne's lanky silhouette sprinting towards her, from behind the cabin. Getting to her feet from the tree against which she was leaning, she prepared herself to take off in either direction. Either towards the cabin, or away from it, depending on what Thorne had to say. Not hearing him fire his gun, she supposed she would have a nice respite at the cabin, very shortly.

"Okay, it's clear," said Thorne with winded breaths.

With quick footing, they made their way towards the small haven. All the while, Thorne's senses on high alert. It was too soon to have Detective Shane crashing his party.

The first thing Tessa did upon walking through the door of the one room cabin, was make a bee line for the tiny bathroom. "I'll be out in ten minutes," she said, quickly closing and locking the door to deny Thorne's acceptance or denial of her statement. She was tired, sore, and hungry, just to name a few, and needed the ten minute solitude to wash this damn day away. Thorne better pray he didn't interrupt her, or the last thing he was going to have to fear, was the damn maniacal masked man. She wasn't in the mood. She would go from demure and cooperative princess, to bat shit crazy on him, in two point five.

Standing with her back against the door, in the small and dark room, she ran her hands along the wall looking for the light switch. The room illuminated to reveal a simple, but effective washroom, complete with a one sink vanity, toilet, and shower. Stripping her soiled clothes off, she stepped into the one person shower enclosure, and let the warm jet of water wash over her. With her arms braced against the wall, and her head hung, she watched the traces of dirt, debris, and blood swirl down the drain.

An epiphany slammed into her like a ton of bricks. Her arms and legs felt as stable as two stretched out rubber bands, as her entire body started to quiver. Was she imagining things, or didn't Thorne say that his car was at the cabin? If it was, then why the hell weren't they in it, getting the fuck out of here? She hadn't seen a car anywhere. Then again, when approaching the cabin, her vision was tunneled right to the front door. Lightly touching her forehead, she felt the large welt, and let the negative thoughts running through her mind get sucked down the drain along with the rest of the filth.

Turning the single levered knob to the off position, she stepped out, and her wet body dripped puddles onto the linoleum tiled floor.

Two steps from the shower, she opened the vanity door, and prayed to the cotton Gods. Yes! The thin and threadbare towel wasn't exactly Egyptian cotton, but it was a towel. After all that had gone wrong, and all that had happened today, it was all she was hoping for.

Redressing in her dirty sweats and t-shirt wasn't exactly what she had in mind, but right now there wasn't any other choice. At least she felt clean beneath her dirty exterior.

Emerging from the bathroom, feeling just slightly refreshed, Tessa was pleased to see that Thorne had set a place for her at the bistro table. He motioned for her to take a seat, and placed a nice and hearty bowl of mac and cheese in front of her. "I know it's not much, but I thought you might prefer a hot meal over a cold peanut butter and jelly sandwich. . . .it's all I could find," he said apologetically.

"No, it's great. Thank you, Bobby." She didn't want to seem unladylike, but she was famished. She was so busy shoveling the elbowed macaroni into her mouth, she didn't notice anything else. Not even the way that Thorne was sitting across from her, taking his time to savor his every bite, and enjoying the show.

*That's right sweetheart. Eat it all up, like a good little girl. Then it's time to go night-night. Forever.* He had ground the sleeping pills up into such a fine dust of powder, that the thick and creamy cheese masked the taste of them. Sure, he could have had some fun with her, like he had with Leopold, but he really wanted to conserve his strength for the real fight.

Swallowing her last mouthful, Tessa offered to clean up.

"Absolutely not," Thorne insisted. "You've been through enough today, Tessa. Why don't you just go lay down on the couch. I'll take care of the dishes, then I'll see if I can get a signal to get in touch with HQ."

"Well, I am getting really tired," she said through a yawn.

"I'm sure you are. You've had a long and exhausting day. Just go rest. I'll take care of everything."

Getting up from the table, and nestling herself onto

the couch, she drifted off comfortably, knowing that since Bobby was calling HQ, this nightmare would be over soon enough.

Thorne took his time cleaning up, and doing the dishes. Within ten minutes, he could hear her slow and deep rhythmic breathing, coming from the other room.

He grabbed his duffle and went out the back door, heading down to the end of the dock. He removed the spool of rope, the roll of duct tape, and the knife. He cut the rope into four pieces of six foot lengths, and carefully laid it all out, in a neat and tidy line up. With high tide coming, it would be all he would need to put this damsel in distress. And Detective Shane too.

# 23. OPEN WATER

DETECTIVE Layne backed the boat trailer down the boat ramp, and into the Gulf with ease. Putting his truck in park, he jumped into the boat from the dock, and eased her off the trailer. She fired right up with no problem. Her double outboard motors purred like a kitty cat. Patting the helm, he said, "Good girl." Once completely off of the trailer, he eased her alongside the dock, and tied her off with a sailors knot. Getting back off the boat, he jumped back into the truck, parked and locked it. Two quick chirps echoed from the truck, in unison with two quick flashes from the head and tail lights.

To some, it might be a little eerie being on the water at night, because it was like an expansive ghost town with no end. At this time of night, there were a few fisherman fishing off the bridge, but there were not very many willing to brave the night sea. Fishing and boating were definitely more popular as  day sports. Detective Layne wasn't spooked in the slightest. He was what is commonly referred to as a "Florida Cracker," meaning he was both born and bred right in Florida. He wasn't a transplant from another state, like most of the rest of the population. He was right at home on the water, since he practically grew up in it, and on it. The light chop swayed the boat slightly, as it rocked against the dock, waiting to ride the open sea.

Detective Layne settled in and checked all the gauges. The dashboard illuminated like a Christmas tree. Everything looked to be in working order. He started slowly heading South in a "no wake manatee zone," when he heard the melody of his ring tone.

"Detective Layne," he answered.

"Hello," the crackled frail voice on the other end questioned.

"Detective Layne," he said again, this time louder, and plugging his opposite ear with a finger.

He turned the key, and cut the power to the boat, because he could not hear too clearly over the churning of the motors.

"Detective Layne," he repeated more loudly.

"This is Nellie Hinkle. I believe you wanted to talk to me?'

Detective Layne sat down in the Captain's chair. "Yes. Yes, Ms. Hinkle. Thank you for calling." *Finally calling*, he thought, but did not say aloud. "Look, Ms. Hinkle, I know it's late, so I don't want to keep you. There is something you need to be aware of though, which is why it was important for us to get a hold of you. Your vehicle, the Lincoln Continental you keep at your residence, here in Naples? It was involved in an accident, and is presently at the NPD being processed for evidence, in connection to an ongoing abduction case.

Hearing Ms. Hinkle gasp, Detective Layne carried on. "Ms. Hinkle, I'm sorry for the news, but your insurance should take care of it. What we need to know from you is, was there anyone that had access to your home or vehicle? Our investigation revealed there were no signs of forced entry into your home or garage. The ignition switch in the car was also not damaged, and the car was not hotwired, which leads us to believe that whoever was driving your car had a key to both the car and your home."

"Well, good heavens," she spoke in her Jersey accent. "I do have someone check on my house, and start my car occasionally while I'm gone over the summer. It couldn't be him that's involved in this though. He's such a nice boy. Why, you probably know him. He's a cop too."

Even though they were operating under the assumption that it might possibly be an inside job, Detective Layne still would have fallen over had he not already been sitting down, because deep down, you never want to think it could be one of your own. A sick feeling punched him in the gut. He stood up, and began pacing the length of the gently swaying boat. He stopped abruptly, with one hand on the phone, the other rubbing his short goateed chin in nervous energy.

Several moments passed in silence, while he gained his thoughts and composure. Detective Layne ran his hand through his long dark locks, and asked the question he was not sure if he wanted to hear the answer to. "What's his name?"

"There has to be some sort of mistake, Detective. I just don't believe that Bobby would ever be involved in anything like that," she said.

"Bobby," he asked. "You mean Bobby Thorne?"

"Why, yes. So, you do know him," she said excitedly. "He's such a nice boy."

"Yeah," he said grimly. "I know him. Thank you, Ms. Hinkle. We'll be in touch."

Detective Layne hit the end button on his cell phone.
"I knew there was a reason I didn't like that motherfucker. I'm gonna throttle that piece of shit," he
mumbled under his breath. He quickly shot out a group
text to Detectives Shane and Wilshire, and to his
Lieutenant, informing them of his newfound
information. It wasn't proven conclusive evidence that
it was Thorne, but it damn sure in hell was looking that
way. He always thought that guy was kind of shady.
Detective Layne bumped the ignition key, and made
his way out of the no wake zone. The compact disc
player's small motor whizzed and  turned to change
tracks. Pantera's "Cowboys From Hell" started
playing. Layne cranked it up, and bobbed his head to
the beat.
"Oh, Hell yeah," he said aloud to himself. "I can
stand some good musical motivation."
Once in open waters, he palm shifted the throttle to
its full open position. Under the inky blackness of the
Gulf, the two outboard motors were whining, being
pushed to their limit. The motors were so quickly
propelling Detective Layne across the moonlit waters,
the boat's bow was barely sheeting over the glass top
surface of the water. He braced himself behind the
helm, as the wind whipped his long locks, and the salty
overspray of the sea encrusted his moistened skin.
Detective Layne readied his ship, and guided her
wheel solely with his left hand. With his other hand, he
held the high powered binoculars that he was using to
periodically scout the shoreline to his East.
His shore view went from viewing the second home
multi-million dollar mansions that dotted the coastal
perimeter of Marco Island, to the small and old Florida
style stilt homes, and shack like cabins that lined the
coastal area further South, towards Everglades City.
In order to give him more time to scout the shore
during his passing, Detective Layne shifted the throttle
to half power, and turned the compact disc player off.

Other than seeing a few night fisherman, it seemed to
be fairly quiet.

Detective Layne was suddenly thrown back, as the
boat hit a large object in the water. Had he not been
busy scouting the shoreline, he may have seen what the
object was, and could have possibly avoided it. He was
very familiar with the area, and knew it was not a
sandbar. His left hand couldn't hold onto the steering
wheel through the force of the impact. As the boat
launched into the air, gravity took over, and Layne's
grip was ripped from the wheel as he was thrown to the
back of the boat. Now airborne, Layne's motion came
to an abrupt halt when his back collided with the deck
of the boat. He scrambled to his feet as the boat was
descending back towards the water, and was trying to
get back to the controls before the boat came down
hard, and ejected him. A few mere moments before the
boat made a second impact with the water, Layne was
able to make it back to the controls to cut the motor,
and brace the steering wheel with both hands. The boat
motors stopped whirling, and the boat hit the water
with a jarring impact. As the warm salt water sprayed
up beyond the sides of the boat, Layne was able to stay
on his feet and maintain control of the water craft.

His first thought was that he had hit a manatee, or
possibly a pilot whale. Recently, pods of the whales
had been coming into the shallower waters, and dying.
Marine biologists couldn't figure out why. Several
times they had moved the whales back out into the
deeper water, just to have them come back in again.

Layne released his white knuckled grip from the
steering wheel, and paced around the perimeter of the
boat. Leaning over each side, he thoroughly scanned
his eyes over the surface of the water. Not initially
seeing anything, he returned to the helm. His hand
gripped the ignition key, and he spoke a silent quick
prayer before turning the key. The engines did not fail
him, as both props churned the water like hot knifes

slicing through butter.

He steered the boat in a wide and inward moving circular pattern. Spotting a black mass in the water, he pulled the boat up along side it and cut the engine. Taking his flashlight, he shined the beam down into the water. "Oh, fuck," he said, as he spotted the lifeless body of a man, floating face down. He quickly realized that what he hit was a person, not a manatee or a pilot whale. Reaching over the side of the boat, he leaned over as far as he could, and stretched his arm out to its limit. His fingertips barely reached the floating, lifeless mass.

In a panic, he scanned the boat and spotted a fishing gaff. Grabbing it, he used the handle end, not the business end, to pull the person in closer. The body came to rest against the edge of the boat. Layne fisted a wad full of flannel shirt in his hand, and floated the limp, downward facing body towards the back of the boat. Upon getting it there, he lowered the dive ladder, gripped with both hands, and heaved.

The man was heavy, but Layne was able to get him onto the deck of the boat with a second try. The lifeless body landed on the deck with a thud, as a wave of water splashed over Layne's shoes and pant legs. Placing the man on his back, Layne immediately saw the clean slice running through the man's neck and quickly assessed that the poor dude was dead long before he hit him with the boat. Judging the rigidity of the body, Layne knew that he hadn't been dead long. He knelt down, and rolled the body towards him to check the pockets of his khaki cargo pants. Feeling his back left pocket, Layne pulled out a tan wallet.

Opening the wallet and pulling out the Florida driver's license, Layne said, "Sonny Holden, huh? Well, Sonny, I'm sorry I wasn't here sooner, unless you're the asshole I'm out here looking for." Placing the license back into the wallet, Layne replaced the wallet where he found it. Taking his hand, he ran it over Sonny's face to close his opened eyes. "Rest in peace, Sonny," Layne said somberly.

Layne returned to the helm, bumped the ignition, and grabbed the wheel. Judging from the direction of the wind, Sonny must have been killed further South. His fresh corpse carried North by the current.

Wanting to make sure he didn't miss anything, or hit any other bodies that might be possibly floating in the water, he moved along the coast at wake speed. He kept his eyes glued to the binoculars for any signs of movement, or anything suspicious.

Spotting a worn dock behind a small cabin up ahead, Layne focused his binoculars in and around that area. "Jesus Christ," he exclaimed, as he set the binoculars down, and eased the throttle forward.

Layne killed the engine before he reached the dock, and drifted up next to it. He had spotted Tessa tied to one of the docks support posts. Her head lulled unconsciously limp, with the rising tide lapping just below her shoulders. In a matter of twenty more minutes, she would drown in the rising tide.

He had to fight his instincts, that were pushing him to jump into the water to free her, but it was a stupid plan. He would get her out of there more quickly if he had something to cut her binds with.

Spying a fish gutting knife surrounded by a pool of blood on the dock, Layne put two and two together to figure out that this must have been where Sonny met his demise. If Sonny ended up in the water with his throat slit, and Tessa was here bound, that could only mean one thing. The psycho was still at large.

Layne jumped off the boat and onto the dock to retrieve the knife. He could use it to cut the rope. He prayed to the Heavens up above that he wasn't too late. Hopefully she wasn't slit like his friend on the boat here.

As Layne squatted down to pick up the knife, he heard quick rushing footfalls coming towards him from the start of the dock. Palming the business end of the knife in hand, he stood erect, keeping it concealed by tucking his arm tight to his leg, and turning the backside of his hand to face outward.

Detective Thorne had his gun drawn, and pointed at Layne. "You," he questioned. "What the fuck are you doing here," he asked, with and emphasis on the word, "you."

With the same emphasis, and without skipping a beat, Layne responded with the exact same words, that had an entirely different meaning with the way they were spoken. "The more appropriate question here, Thorne, is what the fuck, are you doing here?"

Smirking, Detective Thorne said one word. "Revenge."

*Revenge*, Layne thought. *What the fuck is he talking about, revenge?* It was clear to Layne that Thorne was not interested in having a Dr. Phil sit down discussion about it, considering he had a gun pointed at him. Doing the only thing he could think of as a distraction tactic, Layne quickly yelled, "Hey, Lenny, I got him over here," while peering around Detective Thorne. It was all that he could come up with, that would give him a split second advantage.

Detective Thorne turned his head for a brief moment, and realized that Layne was just bluffing. In that brief moment, Layne threw the knife towards Thorne's trigger hand. As the knife was sailing through the air, Thorne turned back towards Layne. Just as the blade of the knife caught the back of Thorne's hand, he jerked, which threw off his aim, but he managed to squeeze off two successive shots.

# 24. CONFRONTATION

LENNY saw a soft pool of flickering light spilling from a small window, in the not too far off distance. With a closer look, he saw another more harsh light bobbing at a farther distance, combined with the faint humming of a motor. His targets had to be somewhere close. His Timex said he had 5 hours left. He knew that in these types of games, it always came down to the wire, so he was willing to bet that the Lincoln crashed on the side of the Alley wasn't in the initial plan. His adrenaline levels spiked at the realization that this was nearing the end of the line, and he allowed the toxic fuel of anger and revenge to take over him. It was either that, or sob like a damn baby. He would stave the sobbing off until Tessa was back in his arms. For now, he'll take anger and revenge, thank you very much. It is much more conducive to thumping someone's ass, and he needed to be in ass thumping mode, right quick. He wanted to yell at the top of his lungs, as the anger built up pressure inside of him, like a pent up volcano. Thinking better of it, he set his duffle down, and performed some martial arts katas to work off the steam and center himself. Better to get the rage out now, than to have it overwhelm him at an inopportune moment. He needed to go into this thinking the worst, but hoping for the best of scenarios. He wasn't scared of the fight, he was looking forward to taking his anger out on someone, and excited to put an end to this all. More than anything, he wanted to get his Tessa back home, safe and sound. The psycho better hope she was still alive, or by the time he was finished with him, he would beg for death if she weren't. He would make damn sure of that. At the mere thought of it, the words long, slow, and torturous fired through Lenny's mind.

After several minutes of katas, Lenny's muscles loosened and lengthened.. His heart beat slow and strong. His mind became focused and centered. His breath was deep and slow, almost meditative. With his eyes closed through the motions, he took deep breaths in through his nose, and out through his mouth. The anger and rage lifted off of him, like a weight had been removed from his chest. It was still there, but had been compartmentalized and contained. Finishing his kata, Lenny brought his palms together at his chest, with his fingertips pointing towards the sky, and took a bow, facing the direction of the lights in the distance. He squinted his eyes and glared, as a smirk crossed his lips. The bow was typically made as a sign of respect. It was a habit, as it was made at the end of all kata forms. He, however, had zero respect for this dirt-bag opponent. He would not underestimate him, but he did not respect him. Anyone that did, or was capable of doing the things that this man did, was nothing but a monster, and did not deserve any respect. He was not only a monster, but a coward. An abuser of women? Let's see how this asshole fares against some real competition... a real opponent.

Lenny squatted down, and unzipped his duffle bag. Grabbing a handful of extra gun ammunition, his pockets became weighted with the cylindrical lead, as he dumped it from his fist. Continuing to feel around the bag, he felt the length of rope that he had taken back at the tree by the smoldering campfire. He wound the length of rope around his left palm, careful to leave his knuckles free, like a boxer wraps his in tape, prior to slipping on his boxing gloves. The rope was comfortably snug, but not restrictive. He stuffed the tail end of the rope underneath the rows that had been wound around his palm.

The last thing Lenny did before he closed the duffle bag, was pop a piece of Wrigley's into his dry mouth, before stuffing an unopened pack into his back pocket. The cool and sweet spearmint danced around his taste buds, and coated his throat with each swallow.

Grabbing the duffle handles and standing erect, Lenny quickly scanned the area for a good hiding spot. Settling on a dense cluster of palmettos, he placed the duffle deep within the bowels of the vegetation to concealed it. Now was the time he needed to move unencumbered by the weight and bulkiness of the bag.

Lenny moved as stealthily as a cat, towards the flickering light. Taking full advantage of his environment, he used the tree trunks as cover. Moving from one to the next, the light grew closer and brighter, until the cabin was about a half mile away, but in clear view.

Hearing a gun shot pierce the night's silence, Lenny's pulse started to race. His arms and legs pumped up and down, back and forth, quickly closing the distance between him and the cabin.

#

The first shot caught Layne in the upper left triceps. Good. Not his trigger arm. He did not feel the chunk of flesh that was ripped from him through the river of adrenaline that was coursing through his veins. The second shot was a complete miss. Right after the first shot connected, at the precise moment Thorne jerked from the pain of the penetration of the knife into his hand, Layne ran full speed at him. Their bodies fiercely collided. Layne grabbed the wrist of Thorne's trigger hand, did a one eighty degree turn, and gave him an elbow smash to the face. Thorne's head snapped back, and blood sprayed from his nose. Thorne's gimp hand released the gun, as he fell to one knee. Layne kicked the gun towards the beginning of the dock. He pulled the knife from Thorne's hand, and tossed it back down towards the end of the dock, where he had come from.

Not being one to give up a fight, Thorne sucker punched Layne right between the legs. Layne instantly released Thorne's wrist, and bent over with both arms cradling his shooting pain soaked abdomen. Thorne scrambled back from where he came, to get his gun. Layne closed in quick behind him, and bear tackled him before he got a chance to pick it up. The two men went flying into the grassy yard area, and the fight was on. Layne could have easily pulled his gun on him, but wanted to get in a few licks of his own. He deserved that much from getting punched in the family jewels, and for getting his new tattoo fucked up with a bullet graze. This asshole deserved a couple of pops, not only for his own satisfaction, but for his fallen comrade, Detective Kate Leopold. And for Tessa. *Shit, Tessa*, he thought. In the midst of all the action, he almost forgot that she was teetering perilously close to drowning, if she wasn't already gone. He was going to have to make this quick.

As the two man roll came to a stop, they separated
and stood facing each other with their hands in boxing
position. Thorne already looked terrible. The blood
flow from his nose had receded, but it was all over his
mouth, chin, and shirt. Layne took a swing at Thorne's
weak spot, his already bloodied busted nose. Bobbing
his head out of the path of the swing, Thorne stepped
in to take a shot at Layne's abdomen. He connected,
and it wasn't anything to laugh about, but Layne's rock
hard abs absorbed the blow. On the retraction of his
fist, Thorne shook off the sting, because it felt like he
hit a cement block. Layne grabbed him in a headlock,
and gave him a good kidney punch. He felt Thorne
grow weak in the knees after that shot. *Good*, Layne
thought. *Now the bastard can piss blood for a week.*
Needing to get out of the headlock, Thorne turned his
head and clamped his teeth down on Layne's arm
flesh. He bit down so hard that he broke skin. Layne
yelled with pain, as he felt Thorne's teeth penetrate
and break his flesh, causing him to let go of the hold he
had on Thorne's head. The two of them squared off,
walking in a circle, cunningly calculating what each of
their next moves would be.

Lenny came rushing around the corner of the cabin.
Confusion set in at the sight that he was seeing. Pulling
his pistol from the holster, he trained it between the
two of them.

Both men stepped out of arms reach of each other.

Thorne pointed at Layne. "Detective Shane, shoot
him. I caught him. He's the one that abducted Tessa."

"Oh, fuck that, bro," Layne responded, throwing his
hands up in disgust. "Lenny, it's not me, it's him. You
know me, man. You know I would never do anything
like this. To you, to Tessa, ...to Katy."

Lenny glanced down towards the ground. He knew
instantly, without question which one of them was
telling the truth. Without taking his eyes off of Thorne,
Lenny sheathed his gun. Slowly closing the distance

between the three of them, Lenny turned to Layne,
"Layne, is my wife alive?"

"She's still alive, Lenny, but she doesn't have much
time left" he said.

"So she's not safe," Lenny asked.

"Not yet, Lenny, but she can be if you got this," he
said.

"Oh, I got this," Lenny said with a hot flash of rage in
his voice.

Lenny grabbed Thorne by the throat with one hand.
Layne took that as his cue to move double time to get
Tessa out of the water. Layne ran down the dock as
fast as his legs would carry him.

Stooping to pick up the knife, as he ran past it. With
the handle firmly in his grasp, he jumped in the water
feet first. Putting the handle of the knife in his mouth,
he had to take about ten strokes to reach Tessa. Diving
down into the water, he started sawing through the
ropes from the bottom up. She was still unconscious,
and he didn't want her unnecessarily falling forward
while he was still working under water. By the time he
got to the last of the ropes, the water had risen to the
bottom of her chin. Five more minutes, and she would
have not been so lucky. Layne cut the last rope, and
turned her over onto her back. He nestled her chin
underneath his elbow to keep her head above water,
and hauled her back to the boat. Getting her up onto
the deck was much easier that getting Sonny up there,
because she weighed a lot less. Once on deck, he
hoisted her over his shoulder, and took her to the front
of the boat. He gently sat her in the captains chair, and
pulled the tape from her mouth. She was still warm,
and her clothes weren't soaked in blood. Good sign.
Gently tapping her cheeks, he called to her, "Tessa.
Tessa. Tessa, wake up."

A moan escaped her lips, and her eyes fluttered open.
Layne grasped her by the chin and held eye contact
with her. "Tessa, you're going to be safe now. Me and

Lenny are here."

"Lenny," she asked in bewilderment.

"Yes, Lenny is here," Layne said. Starting the boat, he said to her, "I want you to take the boat and move offshore a little. If anything goes wrong, you get out of here, understand?"

Layne could tell that she was still quite shaken. "Tessa, don't look at the back of the boat. There is a man back there. I found him in the water."

Tessa's eyes went wide. "Okay, okay," she stammered. "Don't look in the back of the boat," her voice quivered.

Layne's feet landed solidly on the dock, as Tessa started to pull away.

#

Thorne grasped both of his hands around Lenny's wrist and squeezed, in an attempt to loosen the choke hold.

Lenny's face contorted with a twisted anger as he spoke on word through his gritted teeth. "Why?"

Through gasping breaths, Thorne managed to get a word out. "Choking."

Lenny couldn't help himself, he needed to know the answer to his question. He threw Thorne by his neck, to the ground.

"Talk," Lenny demanded.

Thorne was coughing and loud drags of air were being sucked into his lungs as he tried to catch his breath.

"My real name," Thorne said in a raspy voice, "is Bobby, or more properly, Robert Verde, Jr."

Lenny's eyes grew wide, then narrowed with a slight bit of confusion, as his brows furrowed.

Thorne continued on. "When I was growing up, my Mom wasn't around. She left when I was four years old. She was a junkie bitch whore. It was just me and

my Dad. When I was eight years old, YOU put my
Dad in prison. I didn't have anywhere else to go, so I
was bounced through the system." Thorne's voice
started to escalate with rage, "Foster home after foster
home. You have no idea what it was like," he yelled.
" I was beaten, starved, and abused, and it was all
YOUR fault. You needed to pay for what you did to
me, for what you took from me." Regaining his
composure, and lowering his voice, Thorne said,
"Taking my Dad away from me made my life a living
hell Lenny, so here I am to take away what you love."
Looking over at the water, Thorne saw that Layne was
able to get Tessa untied and to safety. Locking stares
with Lenny, Thorne snarled, "You may have gotten
lucky this time, but you won't be so lucky next time."

Thorne should have shut up while he was ahead.
Lenny actually felt sorry for him, but only for a
minute. He wasn't sorry for putting Robert Verde
Senior, serial murderer, in prison, but he did feel sorry
that his parent's actions and lifestyles ended up ruining
the kid's life. It was disheartening that he had
projected his displaced anger onto Lenny, when if
anything, he should have projected these feelings of
rage and anger towards his Mother and Father. Clearly,
he was a psychopath. Like Father, like Son.

Hearing Thorne's spoken threat made Lenny snap,
and his empathy disappeared. "Get up," Lenny
ordered.

Throne scrambled to his feet, with his fists clenched.

"You mad at me, Thorne,… or Verde,… or whatever
the fuck your name is," Lenny pried. "Then be a man,
and you take it out on me. Right here, right now. It's
you and me. Guess what? I'm mad at you too, so this
will be fun for me." Lenny started to remove his guns
and his knife, pitching them behind him. "See. Fair
fight," he said while holding his hands up, his elbows
bent at ninety degrees, palms splayed open, and facing
Thorne. Normally, Thorne wouldn't have been a well

matched opponent to Lenny's skills, but because he
was tired and weak, hungry, and half dehydrated, they
were an equal match. Thorne looked as though he had
already taken a pretty good licking to the nose, but
Lenny wasn't sure exactly what kind of condition he
was in. Lenny did know one thing for sure, and that
was that crazy could give you some powerful energy.

Something clicked in Thorne's head. Maybe Lenny
was right. Maybe he should take it out on him. Lenny
didn't love anything else in this world more than his
wife. What could be worse than causing his wife to
live with pain and sorrow, even if Lenny was no longer
around to know about it. Just the satisfaction of
knowing he got the last laugh was good enough for
him.

Thorne didn't say a word, as he threw his arm
forward and released a fistful of dirt into Lenny's face,
and charged in at him like a linebacker, catching
Lenny off guard. Thorne tucked his head down and led
in with his shoulder catching Lenny around the waist,
pushing him back about fifteen feet. Lenny fell to the
ground onto his back, his eyes blurred and stinging
from the gritty debris. Thorne jumped on top of him
and got in a few punches. Lenny bucked up, and
brought his legs up in a crisscross, anchoring them
tightly around Thorne's neck. Pushing down with his
legs, Lenny was able to get Thorne off of him, and get
to his feet.

Using his shirt sleeve, Lenny drug the cloth across his
eyes. His vision became clearer, but his eyes were
watering excessively, in a desperate attempt to remove
the remaining foreign dirt particles.

Lenny stepped in with a quick left right jab to the
torso. Thorne countered with a fake left jab, followed
by a big roundhouse punch with his right. The cracking
sound echoed through Lenny's head, as Thorne's fist
connected with his ear, snapping his head and neck to
the side. A loud ringing sounded from Lenny's aching

eardrum, and his equilibrium was thrown off, making him dizzy. Lenny stumbled back a few steps, and shook his head trying to get his bearings.

Wanting to end the fight, Lenny mustered up his last bit of energy. He let Thorne continue to walk closer to him. When he got in range, Lenny took a step forward, jumped in the air and did a quick one eighty pivot, fiercely landing a hard roundhouse kick to Thorne's head. Lenny landed back on the ground, firmly on both feet, back into his fighting stance. Thorne went flying, landing on the unkempt grass. He rolled over onto his belly, and got up on all fours. Crawling away from Lenny a brief distance across the yard, he scrambled for Lenny's gun. Before Lenny realized what was happening, Thorne hastily swung around, and fired a shot. Feeling the hard impact of the bullet, Lenny looked down, and clutched his chest. He stumbled backwards, and fell with a thud, onto the ground. Looking up at the star filled sky, he struggled to breath. *Son of a bitch that hurt,* he thought.

As Lenny lay there, Thorne approached him, still pointing the gun. He was so engrossed in the moment, that he didn't notice that there was no blood oozing from Lenny's chest, thanks to the bullet proof vest he was wearing. He didn't hear Layne approaching him from behind, who at up until this point, stood at the end of the dock as a spectator to the brawl. Lenny had said, he had it under control, and Layne didn't want to interfere with Lenny's moment. Once the gun was fired, and the tables were turned, Layne no longer cared if Lenny got pissed at him or not for jumping in.

Thorne was standing at Lenny's feet, and cocked the gun for a second shot. "I win," he gloated. A split second before Thorne's itchy trigger finger could get the shot off, Layne ducked around in front of him, and clocked him hard in the jaw with a solid right. Thorne's eyes fluttered and rolled back into his head. Losing all consciousness, his body collapsed into a

crumple, after being walloped with the knock out
punch. Layne pried the gun from Thorne's grip.
Rolling Thorne over onto his stomach, he cranked his
arms behind his back, and slapped some cuffs on him.
Layne gave him a swift kick, literally in the ass, just
for good measure, and again for fucking up his brand
new tattoo.

"No, we win, you sick fuck," Layne said.

Layne kneeled down beside Lenny, who had
unbuttoned his shirt to reveal the butt end of a bullet
lodged in his vest. Lenny said, "I told you I got this."

Layne shook his head. He stood and offered Lenny a
helping hand. "Fuck you, dude," he said with a smile
on his face.

"I got this," Layne said with an emphasis on "I."
Layne turned towards the water, pointing at the boat
that was drifting just offshore." Your missus awaits,"
he continued.

Lenny winked at Layne, and gave him a big smile.
"Thanks for having my back, man."

Layne extended his hand, and Lenny took it. There
hands gripped, and they pulled each other close and
patted one another on the back.

Layne said, "Anytime, brotha. Anytime… Hey,
Lenny, before I let you go see your wife, I gotta know,
how did you know? How did you know it was him and
not me?"

Lenny said, "your shoes. I tracked the son of a bitch
all the way here. All I had to do is look down at your
feet. Motherfucker's feet are as big as a damn skunk
ape."

Layne smiled and had an "a-ha" moment spread over
his face. "Good work, Detective. Good work. Now, go
see your wife."

Lenny offered his hand to Layne, and they shook
again. Lenny's eye's filled with empathy. "I'm sorry
about Katy, Layne. I know how fond you were of her."

Layne nodded his head. "Thanks, but you were too.

It's a tragic loss for both of us. For all of us. Now go, before I have to kick your ass too."

Lenny smirked, and turned to go to Tessa. He knew in his heart that Layne would be okay in time. And he would too.

As Lenny was running towards the dock, Detectives Wilshire and Lt. Whitten came careening around the corner with guns drawn. Detective Layne looked at them casually, and said, "Oh, hi guys. Glad you could make it, although, you're a little late to the party."

Wilshire and Whitten holstered their guns. Walking over towards Layne and the beaten and unconscious Thorne, Wilshire said, "What the hell happened here?" Turning towards Whitten he said, "looks like we did miss a good party, Lieutenant."

"Looks that way," she said.

Layne gave them the rundown of the nights events. Lieutenant Whitten gave him permission to write up his official report on Monday. It was a direct order from his Lieutenant to take the rest of the weekend off.

#

Lenny's legs didn't stop pumping. They carried him across the grass, onto the wooden dock. Approaching the end of the dock, his feet sprung him up and away from it, as he jumped and did a swan dive right into warm ocean. Surfacing, he took a breath, continuing to kick his legs, while adding a breast stroke. The immense saltiness of the water burned his eyes and his arm, but he didn't give two shits.

Tessa saw him coming, and drove wake speed to meet him halfway. Turning off the ignition, she dropped the anchor. If the boat's deck would have been long enough for her to break into a full speed sprint, she would have. Dropping the ladder at the rear of the boat, she offered her hand, to help Lenny onto the deck.

As his soaking wet body, pressed against hers, they both started shaking and crying. "Oh, Tessa," he sobbed. "I'm so sorry, baby. Thank God you're okay." With her arms securely locked around his waist, he placed his palms on both sides of her face and planted a million kisses. On her forehead, on her cheeks, on her lips.

Giving him a tighter squeeze, and leaning her head into his chest, she didn't need to say anything. Lenny placed one arm around the small of her back, and with his other, he cradled her head, holding it right where she laid it.

After a few moments had passed, Lenny lifted Tessa's chin and said, "This day did not go at all like I planned, but I will completely make it up to you tomorrow, I promise. Happy Anniversary, sweetheart."

Tessa gave him a peck on the lips, and said, "Happy Anniversary, babe. I don't know what you had planned, but I have all that I need. I have my life, I have my health, and I have you."

Giving her a kiss on the forehead, Lenny said, "I love you, Mrs. Lenny Shane."

Pulling her head back, Tessa said, "You know what, Mr. Shane? Scratch that last remark about having everything I need or want, because I could really use a pizza and some beer. I'm starving," she joked.

Lenny chuckled and said, "You drive a hard bargain, but you got yourself a deal. I don't know where we're gonna find a pizza joint open at this early hour of the morning, but by time we get everything sewed up here, and get back home and cleaned up, maybe we can go for lunch?"

"It's a date," she said through a grin.

Lenny saw Layne, Wilshire, and Lt. Whitten standing around Thorne, who was still lying on the ground. He had probably regained consciousness by now, which would explain why Layne was standing there with one of his feet resting on the top of Thorne's back.

"I guess we better get back," Lenny said, as he looked over. "Everyone has had a long night, and they probably want to be getting home. I know I do."

"Come on," he said to Tessa as he grabbed her hand. They walked to the helm of the boat, and Lenny took the wheel. Getting to the dock, he tied off, and waited for the rest of the crew to board.

Lieutenant Whitten walked in front, while Wilshire and Layne escorted Thorne from both sides. Boarding the boat, Layne sat Thorne at the very rear, and cuffed him to Sonny's lifeless corpse.

Lieutenant Whitten sat in the front passenger's chair, and Tessa sat in the captain's chair. Lenny stood at the wheel. Detectives Wilshire and Layne parked their rumps on the edge of the boat, directly across from Thorne.

The sunrise laid a soft orange glow on the water.

As the wind whipped through their hair, Lenny captained the boat over the glass-like water. He unbuckled the leather strap on his Timex, that was continuing it's countdown.

Two hours and winding down. He balled it up in his right hand, and glanced over at his honey. He made a pitch that would have made Babe Ruth strike out. He watched as it sailed through the morning sky, and hit the Gulf in a soft kerplunk, where it would sink to the bottom, and be forgotten.

During the ride back, Layne noticed Thorne glaring a hole into Tessa's back. "Hey," Layne exclaimed, as he smacked Thorne open handed across the face, "don't you look at her."

A short time after that, Detective Wilshire said and did the exact same thing, except he was not referring to Tessa, he was referring to Lieutenant Whitten.

Layne gave Wilshire a funny sideways glance.

"What," Wilshire asked. "He was looking at her," he said unapologetically.

Layne just shook his head and chuckled under his breath. "Okay," he said.

The ride back to the boat launch, and Layne's truck, went otherwise without incident.

# 25. BREAKING NEWS

VERDE finished his second smoke, and snuffed it out by stuffing it into a diet soda can. He was a lot of things, but a liter bug was not one of them.

He had no idea where they were, because he had been down in the cabin the whole time. Walking over to the edge of the bed, Blondie started to quake even more. "Oh, relax, Blondie. I've had my fill of you. For now. Where are we?"

Pulling the sheet up even more, and staring at the wall, she said, "About twenty-five miles off the coast." She did not want to look into the eyes of the man that just violated her in the most intimate way.

"Anyone else around here," he said, waving his finger in a circle.

"I don't think so," she spoke quietly. "You've had

your fun, now will you let me go? Please," she
pleaded.

"Fun," he razzed. "Blondie, I haven't had any fun
yet. Trust me, you'll know when I do."

Blondie started to weep. "Are you going to kill me?"

Verde snickered to himself, and said, "you stay here,
and don't do anything stupid. I'll be right back." *Was
this bitch dumb, or what? No, honey, I'm not going to
kill you. I've only assaulted you, and let you see my
face. And, I'm an escaped convict, which she wasn't
aware of. Of course, I'm going to kill you. Some people
were so dumb.*

Blondie watched as Verde pulled something small
and shiny out of a beach bag that was not hers, then
exited the cabin, onto the deck of the boat. The precise
moment the door closed behind him, she scrambled off
the bed. Opening the top bureau drawer, she furiously
rooted through it, and pulled out a t-shirt and a pair of
blue jean shorts. From the top of the bureau, she pronto
grabbed a lighter, and stuffed it into her front pocket.
She didn't smoke, but had kept a lighter on the boat, to
light candles. With her bare feet racing across the teak
wood floor, she went into the bathroom and grabbed a
can of hairspray.

She could hear Verde walking around the perimeter
of the boat, on the deck above. She stationed herself to
the left of the stairs, and waited. Hearing the cabin
door swing open, and footsteps descending the stairs,
her heart started to hammer, as her panic reached an all
time high. She readied the lighter in one hand, and the
hair spray in the other.

As Verde reached the second to last step, he noticed
that Blondie was no longer in the bed. Stepping onto
the last stair, he turned to look towards the bathroom,
figuring she was in there trying to wash his filth off of
her body.

Blondie turned towards him, flicked the bic, and
pressed the nozzle of the hairspray. A blow torch flame

hit Verde right in the face. The nauseating smell of burning flesh and hair consumed the cabin. As he started yelling in pain, his hand lost grip on the small cutting tool he was holding, to cup and shield his now fried mug. Blondie's mouth gaped wide as she watched the sharp instrument hit the floor. She wasted no time shoving him out of the way, and jetted up the stairs, taking two at a time.

Climbing the stairs in record speed, she emerged onto the deck, and slammed the door shut. There was no time to find anything to prop up against the door to keep him inside. Running over to the instrument panel, she took a quick look at the compass, to see which direction they were facing. There was a light wind, so it was possible that the boat could have turned since she anchored it.

She raced across the deck of the boat, and dove off the back, into the salty, cool dark water. She had never swam so fast before. Without looking behind her, she kept a fast pace, and a steady stroke. Her only chance of survival would be to get to an uninhabited Key that was about a half-mile towards inland, without getting caught.

#

Verde's hands were trembling as he reached for the knob to open the cabin door. Partly because he didn't know if Blondie would ambush him again with a fire facial, but mostly because of the pain. He grabbed the knob and slug the door open. Peeking his head out quickly, he didn't see her standing there. He emerged onto the deck cautiously. Roaming the deck of the boat, he looked in all possible places for her to hide. Son of a bitch, she wasn't there. Doing a three sixty, Verde surveyed the endless expanse of blue. Scratching his head, he wondered, where the fuck did she go?

She obviously jumped ship. Not knowing in which direction she went, Verde decided it was time to get the hell out of Dodge. If they were twenty-five miles off the coast like she said, then the Atlantic would take care of her anyway.

Descending back into the cabin, Verde walked into the bathroom to take a look at the damage. His face was plenty red, but the flesh wasn't dripping or peeling off. His eyebrows had been singed, but not completely. With some time, some sun burn relief spray, and a nice couple of gallons of Aloe, he would be fine. He rooted through the medicine cabinet, and softly winced while applying a topical treatment.

The hot sting dissipated almost immediately, as his skin glistened with a petroleum shine.

#

Several hours later, the boat was docked, and Verde was in a Naples townhouse, comfortably stretched out on a sofa, watching the nightly news. Bobby should be home at any time now. They had a lot of catching up to do. With his son, the cop, on his side, he could now stay one step ahead of the police. His eternal freedom was eminent. They had already discussed leaving the country together. Bobby said that he had taken care of everything. New identities, complete with fake birth certificates, passports, and offshore bank accounts. Expecting to see himself as a top story, he sat up and clicked the remote volume up to hear the latest gossip of breaking news. The remote fell out of his grip, when he saw Bobby's face plastered all over the television.

"What the...," he said, as he leaned in and listened closely to the story of the Naples Homicide Detective that was charged and booked for several accounts of kidnapping, murder, and attempted murder.

"In other breaking news," a brunette reporter continued, "a Miami-Dade woman was rescued off the coast of Miami. She said she was snorkeling, and when she surfaced, she had strayed too far from her boat, because she could no longer see it. In a heroic effort, she swam to the safety of an off mainland Key, where nearby boaters saw her waving for help. She was treated at the hospital for mild exhaustion and dehydration, and was released earlier this evening. She is now resting comfortably at home. The lucky woman declined an interview with us at Fox 7 News. And now, over to Jim Myers for our local weather forecast."

Verde clicked off the TV, and paced around the room. At least Blondie was keeping her mouth shut. Probably due to the fact that she didn't know who he was, and didn't want him coming back. The stuff with Bobby? This called for an intervention. A seriously calculated intervention. He abruptly stopped pacing, and smiled. Looking like a stark raving mad lunatic, he started laughing out loud to himself, as the idea wheel stopped spinning, and came to a winner. It was time to go raid Bobby's closet, and hope that he had some Sunday's best in there.

# 26. SPILLING GUTS

ARRIVING at the boat launch, the team piled into Layne's dual cab truck, leaving Thorne handcuffed to Sonny in the back of the boat, to ensure he wouldn't be going anywhere. They arrived at the station thirty minutes later, with the boat in tow on its trailer.

Thorne was booked and processed, and the Medical Examiner's office was phoned to pick up Sonny Holden for autopsy.

Lieutenant Whitten called for a brief meeting for all of those involved. Moving into the break room, she had a nice spread of donuts and muffins, waiting for them. The scrumptious sweets filled their empty bellies, and between the five of them, they washed it all down with several pots of freshly brewed coffee.

Tessa sat on the black leather sofa, and flipped

through magazines during the meeting. The rest of them sat around the break room table, discussing what and what not to put into their official reports.

The entire meeting took only about fifteen minutes. Lieutenant Whitten dismissed the team, but not before giving Lenny a week off with pay.

As everyone stood, Lieutenant Whitten said, "Not you, Wilshire. I need to speak with you in private."

Detective Wilshire glanced around the room. "Okay, Lieutenant," he said, as he pulled his chair back out and took a seat.

Layne and Wilshire glanced at each other, and Wilshire shrugged his shoulders.

As the team left the room, Manny Sanchez was waiting at the door. "Lieutenant," he called. "Can I speak with you for a quick minute?"

Looking at Wilshire, Lt. Whitten said, "Give me just a minute. I'll be right back."

"Why are you still here," she questioned, as she and Manny walked to her office. "You should be home enjoying your weekend. We got our man. The rest of the evidence can wait until Monday to be processed."

Manny closed the door behind them. "Sara, I just wanted to let you know that I need to give my resignation. I accepted an offer this morning, with Miami Metro. I start in two weeks. I know that it's probably bad timing right now, with everything you and the rest of the department have just been through, but I needed to tell you. Don't worry, I'll make sure that all of the evidence from this case is handled and processed by me, before I go."

Lt. Whitten felt relieved that a one thousand pound elephant had just been lifted off of her chest. She had to keep herself in check, because she didn't want to seem overjoyed at Manny's news. She really hated to see Manny go, but it was also somewhat of a relief for her, due to personal reasons. *Irrational, selfish, very personal reasons*, she thought. At least now, it wouldn't be so awkward around the station. She wouldn't have to go through giving an explanation to him about her and Wilshire's relationship. Not that she owed him an explanation, but she would have felt obligated to give him one if he were sticking around. That is, if Wilshire wanted to have a relationship. Her stomach turned in knots just thinking about the conversation she was about to have with Wilshire in the other room.

"I appreciate you telling me now," she said. "You're really great at your job, Manny, and they are lucky to be getting you." She gave him a hug, and said, "I wish you nothing but the best. If things don't work out, or if you ever want to come back, you know you are always welcome on my team."

"Thanks, Sara."

She gave him a faint smile. "I'm sorry, Manny, I have to get back," she said, nodding towards the break room.

"Yeah, yeah, of course," he said, as he opened the door for her.

She hesitated as she was crossing the threshold of the door, and turned towards Manny. "Thank you for picking up the refreshments. See you Monday, then," she said, as she lightly touched his shoulder.

"Yeah, Lieutenant," he smiled. "See you Monday."

This wasn't your typical break up, because they were never really together. It was mutually understood between the both of them, that they released each other to move on with their lives, in whatever direction it took them.

Lt. Whitten's heart raced, and her palms were sweating, as she made her way back to the break room. In her head, she was trying to figure out what to say, without looking like a total idiot.

Entering the room, she closed the door behind her. Detective Whitten was sitting calmly at the table, with his hands wrapped around a crisp white coffee mug.

To further avoid the conversation, she walked over
to the coffee pot, and poured herself a mug, topped off
with cream and sugar.

Walking slowly over to the table, she told herself to
quit being so ridiculous, and just spit it out. The worst
he could do would be to reject her. No, on second
thought, the worst scenario would be for him to
intimately schmooze her and use her, then move onto
the next, as per his usual MO. *That* wouldn't make for
an awkward working environment, or anything.

Taking a seat across from him, Whitten began.
"Look, Wilshire…what happened out there, was…"
She had absolutely no idea how to word it, or what to
say. At the time, she thought she felt the reciprocation,
but now, she began to wonder if she was just simply
imagining it.

Detective Wilshire looked intently at her with his
steely green eyes. He reached across the table, and
took her hand in his. "What happened out there, was
amazing. That's the word you're searching for, Sar…
Lieutenant. Everyone around here thinks I'm a …
playboy, … and I guess it does look that way. All of
those girls were just distractions to me. Something to
pass the time, while I waited for what I've really
wanted … all along."

Lt. Whitten's jaw dropped slightly, but nothing came
out. Now she was completely speechless. She glanced
down at his hand, holding hers, then glanced back up
at him.

Detective Wilshire released her hand, stood up, and
walked towards the door. Before turning the handle,
and without turning around, he said, "I'll pick you up
at eight tonight, Lieutenant. Wear something nice. I'd
love to see you in a dress and heels."

He exited the room with a pep in his step, and a smile
from ear to ear. He planned on romancing Sara
Whitten, like she had never been before.

# 27. SURPRISE

THE Mustang's window's were rolled down, as
Lenny and Tessa cruised out of the station, down US
41 towards Palm Drive, with their hands intertwined.
The sun was up, and the warm air blew through their
hair.

They cruised down their palm lined street, and
skidded to a halt, as Lenny flat-out whipped into their
driveway. Hitting the remote automatic garage opener
that was attached to his visor, the squeaky sound of the
rolling door prompted Tessa to say, "You really need
to fix that thing."

"Put it on the list," Lenny said with a wink, as he
pulled the Mustang into the garage, and hit the close
button on the remote. "Lieutenant did give me a week
off with pay, so I'll be waiting for you to hand me my

honey do list," he joked. Hand in hand, they ran into
the house, like a couple of giddy teenagers.

Once inside, they split up, and urgently double
checked to make sure all of the doors and windows
were locked, and all of the shades were drawn. For the
next couple of hours, they wanted to be alone, without
being disturbed. They especially didn't want an
intrusive unwanted visitor to come strolling in, namely
Mr. Perkins.

Tessa finished her side of the house first, and headed
into the master bath. Stripping her clothes off in a mad
frenzy, she left them lay in a pile on the floor. Opening
the frameless glass shower door, she turned the double
full body shower on, and stepped in to the arctic-white
granite enclosure. The coolness of the smooth surface
felt good on her aching feet.

Stepping face first under the shower head, she let the
hot water run through her hair, and over her face, as
she closed her eyes. The body jets soothed every inch
of her aching body, and filled the air with billowing
steam.

She heard the shower door open, and was caressed
from behind. Lenny gathered her hair, and gently
kissed her neck.

His hands massaged her scalp for a notably good five
minutes, in glorious fresh scented bubbles, followed by
another five minute scalp, neck, and shoulder massage
with her hair conditioner.

Spinning her around to face him, Lenny used the
lightest touch to run his fingers over the bruised and
swollen area of her head. "You could use some ice on
this," he said.

"I'll do it later," she said gruffly. "Right now, ice is
not what I need, Mr. Shane."

She leaned in and kissed him deep and frantically.
Lenny responded by locking his lips with hers, hoisting
her light frame up, and holding her straddled legs
around him. With her back to the wall, they became

one.

Tessa let out a moan, as her void was completely filled. Pleasure rippled through both of them, as the steady rhythmic rocking grew to be deeper and faster.

The sound of their bodies slapping together filled the room.

Tessa's body quivered and grew tense, as her love muscles started to contract and release, sending a flow of warm wetness over Lenny's shaft. Her head reared back, as she said breathlessly, "Oh, baby, that feels so good."

Sending Lenny over the edge, his entire body grew rigid, as his throbbing manhood erupted in it's own release.

Lenny let her down slowly, and they shared a loving kiss.

Taking turns washing each other, they finished with their shower, feeling clean, refreshed, and satisfied.

They settled together, into their king sized bed for a nice long nap, wearing nothing but smiles.

#

Several hours later, Lenny and Tessa woke, feeling completely rested. They made love once again, but this time it was more slow and less urgent.

After getting dressed, they headed out on the motorcycle, to grab some lunch.

They walked into Brick Oven Pizza, and Lenny requested to be seated by the hostess in a booth at the back of the restaurant.

He ordered a large meat lover's pizza, and a pitcher of Bud with frosted mugs. The waitress promptly brought the drink order, along with a complimentary basket of fresh out of the oven garlic and parmesan breadsticks with warm marinara.

They sat there in silence snacking on the breadsticks, and sipping the amber ale.

Lenny piped up, "Do you want to talk about it, Tessa?"

She breathed in an audible deep breath, and blew it out. "No, I want to forget about it," she said.

"Okay, you're the boss," he said. "If you change your mind, I'm here. I'll always be here."

"I'm fine, Lenny. Can we change the subject," she said as she smoothed the cloth napkin on her lap.

"Sure," he said. "You were pretty damn smoking hot this morning, Mrs. Shane," he teased.

Tessa let out a giggle, and blushed. Shaking her head, she said, "shut up, Lenny," followed by another giggle.

He looked at her with a twinkle in his eye. "That's the smile I was looking for."

"So," he said in a more serious tone. "While you were getting into the shower this morning, I had to call and reschedule the dinner reservations I had planned for our Anniversary."

Tessa turned her head in curiosity. "Oh," she said quizzically.

"We'll be having dinner tonight, seven o'clock, at Ruth's Chris Steakhouse."

"That sounds fantastic! Thank you, honey," she responded, as she leaned across the booth to give him a peck on the lips. Her taste buds watered at the thought. It was her absolute favorite place to get a nice filet mignon. Melted in your mouth like butter.

"I do have another surprise, that I wanted to give you during our Anniversary dinner. I just can't wait any longer though to give it to you," he said with a frenzied excitement growing in his voice.

"Really," she asked, with anticipation in her voice. "There's more? What is it? What did you get me," she asked in exhilaration.

Lenny nodded his head, as he prolonged her agony. "Oh, you're gonna like this. You're really gonna like this," he said as a large grin consumed his face.

Reaching into his vest pocket, he pulled out a large

business sized envelope, and handed it to her.

She maintained eye contact with him, as she accepted it. "And what might this be," she wondered aloud.

"Open it," he said. It was unclear who was more excited. Lenny to give the gift, or Tessa to receive it.

After taking a couple of gulps from her beer, Tessa tore the envelope open, careful not to rip the contents inside. She pulled out two pieces of tri folded paper, and unfolded them.

Her eyes scanned the paper and read it's contents. "A vacation," she said giddily. "We're actually going to go on a vacation," she asked with enthusiasm.

"We're actually going to go on a vacation," he said with laughter.

She jumped up from her side of the booth, and squeezed in right next to Lenny. Wrapping her arms around his neck, she smothered him with fast, light kisses. "Thank you, honey! I love it, I really love it! I'm so excited," she squealed.

Her face suddenly grew somber. "Wait," she said. "I don't want to get all excited about us going on a romantic getaway, just to have to cancel at the last minute because of one of your cases, like always."

"Well," he sighed. "The thing about this trip is, it's not just for our Anniversary. I thought it would be a really good start for our next chapter."

Looking at him like he had two heads, she hesitantly asked, "What are you talking about?"

Brushing her cheek, he said, "I'm retiring from the department." Her face grew slack, as he continued, "it's time for a different direction for me, Tessa. A direction that we can move towards, together. You know I love my job, but it's my job. It's who I am, who I've grown to be, but you're my world. My life. My everything." Changing to a more jovial voice, he said, "besides, I'd much rather hang around a pretty girl like you all day, than a bunch of criminals and boneheads…and, on top of that, it's not like I can't make  citizen arrests," he laughed nervously.

Tessa laughed at the last statement, because it was funny. Funny because it was probably more truth than not. Grabbing his hand, and gazing into his eyes, she said, "If that's what you want to do, I support you all the way. Nothing would make me happier. Just make sure you're doing it for the right reasons. Don't do this just for me," she pleaded, with the flow of hot tears escaping her eyes.

"Honey," he said, as took his thumbs and wiped the tears from her eyes, "I've thought about this long and hard. I'm doing this because it's what I want. That's the reason. No more, no less."

Tessa became so overwhelmed with happiness, she got choked up, and excused herself to go to the ladies restroom to wash her face. The last thing she wanted was for everyone in the restaurant to think was that she was a bubbly faced victim, and that Lenny was a bad guy that made her cry. Nothing could be farther from the truth. These were tears of joy. He was a great guy, that made her very happy.

While Tessa was off washing her face, the waitress came and delivered a thick crusted, meat topped, gooey cheesed, circular pan of goodness. She dished the first slice onto each of the two plates, and indicated that she would bring another pitcher of beer.

Tessa returned from the restroom with a fresh face. She and Lenny had their fill of pizza and beer, then headed home, both of them satisfied in every way.

## 28. DATE NIGHT

LIEUTENANT. Sara Whitten stood in her bedroom in only a black lacy bra and matching panties. Her auburn hair hung down to the middle of her back in soft loose waves, and her flawless alabaster skin was highlighted with natural looking makeup. She had five different dresses scattered across her bed, along with five different sets of heels strewn around her bedroom. It was the most clutter her monotone minimalist designed bedroom had ever seen. The room was large, but cozy, with it's soft monochromatic color scheme. When designing the room, she had viewed pictures of other monochromatic rooms that looked cold and sterile. To avoid this, she used soft neutrals as opposed to hard, bold, saturated colors. She stuck with soft antique whites, and grays with a hint of blue hue, in varying shades.

Pulling yet another dress from her closet, she held the white and black number up against her, and smoothed it out. Looking at herself in the mirror, she tilted her head from side to side. She slipped it off of the hanger, and onto her body. The dress fit her like a glove, and looked sexy but classy. The white chiffon top clinched just below her breasts, with a high waist thin silver belt, which accentuated her bosom. The remainder of the dress was a black nylon fabric that clung to her curves, and came to just below mid thigh. She opted for a pair of slung back, open toed four inch heels, that showed off her perfect, freshly manicured fire engine red toenails.

Hearing the doorbell ring, she did a quick once over in the mirror, and reapplied her soft pink-pearl lipstick, followed by two quick squirts of her light, floral scented perfume to each side of her neck. Her heels click clacked across the clean white tile. Reaching the door, she placed her shaky hand on the handle. Tonight wasn't going to be just another day at the office. Swallowing hard, and gathering her nerve, she opened the door.

Detective Brian Wilshire's eyes danced with delight. "Wow," he exclaimed. "You look absolutely, utterly stunning!" At the station, he always thought she was pretty in her demure business attire, but he had never seen her look like this. She was the epitome of sexy with her hair down, and her long flowing naked legs showing. And he thought she looked hot in her jeans? Yeah. This was going to be a loooong fucking night. Minus the fucking.

He was looking pretty dapper himself, in his charcoal gray suit and tie. And, he smelled amazing.

*My God, what have I gotten myself into*, she thought.

Handing her a single orchid, he said, "Here, I brought you this."

"Thank you, on both accounts," she blushed. Taking

the orchid, she set it on her coffee table. "Shall we go," she asked.

Detective Wilshire locked arms with her, and proudly escorted her to his car. Like a perfect gentleman, he opened the car door for her, and she settled in to the passenger seat of his sleek Mercedes.

The interior smelled of fine leather, and of the cologne that Wilshire had on. Not an overwhelming sickening smell, but just a hint of it, that made her want to get closer to him just to smell more.

Wilshire sat down in the driver's seat, buckled up, and sat there expectantly looking at her.

"What," she asked.

"Are you going to buckle up?"

"Oh, Jesus," she exclaimed. "Sorry. Don't get me wrong, I want to be here, but this whole situation is weird. Out of my comfort zone," she said, as she grabbed the seatbelt, and strapped herself securely in.

"Don't be nervous, Lieutenant, it's just me," he said, as he eased out of her driveway.

"Okay," she said, "we have to get one thing straight, right off the bat. At the office, on a case, or at a work function, I'm Lieutenant. Here, I'm Sara."

Reaching over to pat his hand on her knee, he said, "Okay. You're the boss, Lieutenant Sara."

A wave of anticipation rose through her with the slightest touch of his hand. Without consciously realizing it, her knees parted slightly. Realizing what her body was doing without her consent, she placed her hands on her knees, and inconspicuously clasped them together.

She smirked and gave him a quick little punch in the arm. "Quit being a smart ass, Brian."

Rubbing his arm, he said with a chuckle, "Ouch. Quit being so abusive, Sara."

They both shared a mutual smile and laughed.

"So, where are you taking me," she inquired.

"Well, I thought we would start with a nice

waterfront dinner at Cloyde's."

Sara knew of Cloyde's, but had never been there. It was often filled with patrons that had money. Lots of it. Under normal circumstances, it was the kind of place where she would have felt like a square peg trying to fit into a round hole. Tonight, however; she felt and looked like a million bucks, so she supposed it was okay. And, even though she didn't have that kind of money, she was with someone that did. Brian Wilshire looked the part, and projected the part, because he was the part. That was one of the things that she really admired about him. He was a damn good, hard working Detective, even though he didn't have to be. He wanted to be. He had inherited a large trust fund from his Grandfather's estate, who was a real estate tycoon over in West Palm Beach. From what she understood, he was pretty much set for life, and would never have to work another day, if he didn't want to.

Arriving at Cloyde's Sara marveled at how beautiful the view of the ocean was through the restaurant's far wall, that was made entirely of glass. The atmosphere was extremely romantic with the view of the ocean, the white linen table cloths, and glowing candle lit table centerpieces. Brian marveled at the view as well, but he was not looking at the ocean. His mouth watered, but it wasn't because of the smell of the five star food.

The hostess welcomed them, and seated them at the far side of the restaurant. At a table for two, they sat against the glass wall, offering them an unobstructed ocean view.

Brian took the liberty of ordering a bottle of Cabernet for the both of them, while they viewed the menu.

Sara didn't really know what to think. The menu had an array of fancy, but fabulous sounding dishes. It also had no prices next to anything, so it must be pretty expensive she thought. She smiled to herself as she remembered an old saying that went something like: if you need to know the price, you can't afford it.

Leaning in, she asked Brian, "what are you going to get?"

"I'm thinking the surf and turf sounds good," he said. "I want you get whatever you want, Sara."

Sara ended up selecting a butter poached lobster tail dish with potato croquets, secretly hoping in the back of her mind, that it was not the most expensive item on the menu.

Sara's taste buds danced in ecstasy, as she and Whitten enjoyed a feast fit for a King and a Queen. They leaned in towards one another as they easily and smoothly conversed, their body language freely telling everyone that they were together. Upon finishing off the entire bottle of Cabernet, Brian leisurely ordered two coffees, and a scrumptious plate of desert berries that came drizzled with white and milk chocolate, which encircled an expertly swirled dollop of crème.

Finishing their desert, Brian placed a black credit card into the check holder the waitress had deposited on their table. After signing the check and leaving the waitress a generous tip, he escorted his lovely date out of the restaurant. Brian was coherent enough to notice that she was catching the undivided attention of all the males, and jealous glares from all of the females, as their companions' heads turned.

Leaving the restaurant, they strolled arm in arm down Fifth Avenue, window shopping, and people watching. Hearing some live music coming from one of the many upscale establishments, they entered and strolled up to the bar. She wasn't drunk, because all of the food she ate seemed to absorb the affects of the alcohol for the most part. She was feeling buzzed, a little loose and a lot giddy. Not wanting to let her inhibitions completely go, she decided to decline having another drink, and opted to have a glass of ice water instead. While this evening had been the best date by far that she had ever experienced, what she really wanted to do was go home. With him. In her bed. Or his. She grew hot, and her cheeks went rosy, as her face flushed just thinking about it.

She snapped out of her daydream, and accepted the ice cold water from the bartender. Brian didn't get anything to drink. He took her by the hand, and twirled her onto the dance floor. They rocked and swayed to the up tempo beat of the jazz band, until last call.

Brian gave her a kiss on the cheek as they exited the dance floor, and strolled down Fifth back to his car.

The ride home was not uncomfortable, as they continued talking and laughing.

Pulling into Sara's driveway, Wilshire exited the car, and opened Sara's door for her. He took her hand, and helped her up and out, continuing to hold it until they arrived at her front door.

Fumbling through her purse for her keys, she pulled them out and said, "Wilshire, I had a fabulous evening. Thank you so much." Hesitating for a moment, she said, "Would you like to come in for a while?"

Wilshire drew her in close and tucked her hair behind her ear. His warm breath tickled her ear, and sent a shiver down her spine as he whispered, "there is nothing more that I would rather do, but if I come in, we both know where it's going to go, Sara. Trust me, it's only out of the respect I have for you, that I won't be coming in tonight."

He grazed his lips across her cheek, from her ear to her mouth, and gave her a light kiss. It left her leaning in and waning for more.

"Goodnight, Wilshire," she said catching her breath.

"Goodnight, Sara," he called, as he walked back to his car.

Sara entered her house, and locked the door. The first thing she did was take off her heels, that were starting to burn at the balls of her feet. The next thing she did was spread her arms and twirl around squealing with delight, like an immature little school girl that just got kissed for the first time.

For the first time ever, Sara had a feeling that this relationship could actually go somewhere.

# 29. THE IDEA

LENNY and Tessa arrived at the beautiful Cancun International Airport, from Miami International, which was only a little over an hour flight. After promptly going through immigration, and collecting their bags at the baggage claim, they headed out of the airport, to the pre arranged hotel transportation.

After forty five minutes of heading South in the stretched white van, they arrived at the Occidental Grande Hotel. Pulling up to the second floor lobby, the driver then removed their luggage from the back of the van, and Lenny tipped him, saying, "Thank you, Amigo."

They entered the expansive open air palapa, and were immediately greeted, being handed one of the hotels signature tropical drinks, and a cool wet cloth. Being from South Florida, the cool cloth was nice, but they were used to the warm and humid weather. They weren't sweltering like their counterparts visiting the hotel from various other regions of the country, where they see more snow than sunshine.

They both marveled at the level of craftsmanship and elegance. The lobby with it's marble floor and open air design, had a beautiful water feature that ran a good length of the entire lobby. At the far end of the lobby, which led to the rest of the hotel, there were two sets of wide staircases, opposite each other, that led down to a natural flowing river. This area featured an entirely lovely shopping strip, and a lobby bar. The furniture was of modern contemporary design, and the vibrant colors of the tropical plants accented it all.

After checking in at the front desk, their bags were taken by the bellman, and they were hand delivered, promptly to their ocean view room, via a stretched golf cart tram.

The room was not small and not large. It was perfect. The Mexican tile complimented the dark wood accent pieces, and tropical decor. Before exiting the room, the bellman gave Lenny and Tessa a map of the property. Looking at it, they saw that it was an expansive, rich ecological reserve, complete with flamingos, monkeys, parrots, and deer.

"Holy shit," Lenny joked, "we better keep a hold of that thing, or we might just get lost."

"I'll keep a hold of it, or else you'll lose it," she joshed.

"Deal," he said. "Now let's go explore this place and find a cold beer somewhere. What do you say, Mrs. Shane?"

"Well, you can have the beer, I want a nice, tropical fruity drink," she said.

The next eight days were filled with relaxation, exploration, rejuvenation, and of course, lots and lots of romance.

On the last night of their stay, they had reservations

for dinner at one of the resort's themed reservation-only restaurants.

They dined on a scrumptious array of Japanese cuisine. During the desert course, Tessa leaned in and gazed into her lover's eyes and said, "Lenny, thank you for this. I have had such a wonderful time. I needed this… We needed this."

Lenny winked at her from across the table and said, "No, thank you, Tessa. Thank you for sticking with me for all of these years. Even when I was always too busy working, and not around much. It was always nice to come home to you. And," he added changing to a more playful tone, "I have also enjoyed myself so much this week, that I think we're just going to have to make this a yearly trip."

"Now, that sounds like a plan," she exclaimed.

"On a more serious note, Lenny, I want to run something by you," she said.

He only nodded his head to indicate for her to continue on, because he had a mouthful of desert.

"Well," she said with hesitation, "I've been thinking about you this week. About your retirement from the force, and I think I've come up with something that you might like."

Swallowing his mouthful, and full of intrigue, he said, "go on."

"Well, what if you were to open a private investigative firm?" She judged his facial expression, and determined that he was still interested in her continuing. She continued on, "this way, you take the cases you want, don't take the ones you don't. You will work for yourself, on your own hand selected cases. Make your own schedule. You'll still kind of be doing what you love to do, but you'll have more time to spend doing other things." Her words were of a more of a non argumentative inquisition, than stated facts.

She was giving him things to think about, and he

seemed to be receptive.

Leaning back in his chair, Lenny took a long sip of his black coffee. Setting the cup down, he ran his hand over his thick mustache to smooth it out. Tessa was looking at him, waiting for him to say something.

"Yeah, I like it. I think that's a fine idea, Tessa. Only one problem I see."

"What's that," she said, pretty excited about his reception to her idea.

"If I'm going to be doing private investigative work, the first thing I'm going to need is a really good photographer. You know one," he asked with a completely serious face.

"Me," she questioned, as she brought her hand up and placed it on her chest. "You want me, to work with you," she said in disbelief. This possibility had never entered her mind, when she devised the idea.

"Why not? You're one of the best damn photographers I've seen. It will give us time together, and who knows, maybe we can find some sort of exciting Mission Impossible type cases," he laughed.

Speechless, she gathered her thoughts and said, "I accept the position, Mr. Shane. Thank you for the offer," she exclaimed.

THE END

# EPILOGUE

SEVERAL weeks later, after giving his retirement notice, Lenny sat behind the cherry wood desk in his second floor, cozy four hundred square foot private-investigative office. It wasn't big, but big enough for a front reception area, a restroom, a small darkroom, and a private office. Thanks to Tessa's decorating skills, the space was homey and comfortable. If it were up to him, he could have sufficed with two chairs, a desk, and a coffee pot.

He stuffed several compromising photos of a married male and an unmarried female, in a plain manila envelope. The work wasn't all that exciting, but it was steady. Surprising how many Wives and Husbands didn't trust their spouses. Funny thing was, usually the majority of them were right not to.

Being a PI certainly had its perks over being a cop.

For instance, he was "allowed" to do certain things that he couldn't do when he was a cop. Things that may have gotten cases thrown out of court. That part, he liked.

He and Tessa had never been closer than now. He loved watching the excitement on her face when they went on a stake out, or on a so called intel fishing expedition. Sometimes they even devised set-ups to see if any bate would be taken. But, he longed for a case that would stimulate his brain. Something he could really sink his teeth into. Something that mattered.

Lenny looked up, as a soft knock came on his door. "Come in."

Lenny smiled and stood to embrace his former boss, Lieutenant Sara Whitten. "Sara! How are you," he asked, as he came around the desk and wrapped his arms around her, kissing her on the cheek.

Lieutenant Sara Whitten returned the gesture, but seemed a little too stiff. Lenny got the feeling this wasn't just a social call or happy hour visit. "What? You're not happy to see me," he joshed.

"Yes," she smiled. "Yes, Lenny, I'm very happy to see you, but I don't think you're going to be all that happy to see me," she said, hanging her head, and looking at the polished terrazzo floor.

Lenny motioned for her to sit, and he walked over to the coffee pot. Sara settled herself in an overstuffed armchair. As he was brewing them some fresh roast Columbian java, he said with his back to her, "Well, before we get to that, let's catch up a little. So...how's everyone doing. I mean," Lenny turned and pointed to her left ring finger, " I noticed that rock you have on your finger, the minute you walked through the door. Damn thing nearly blinded me," he joked. Sara giggled. God she missed being around him everyday. "You know, how the hell do you lift that thing?"

Sara lifted her hand and admired the platinum band

topped with a flawless one carat princess cut diamond. Smiling, she said, "Well, I did have to wear a sling for the first week."

Lenny settled into his chair behind the desk, and set two steaming cups down in front of them. "Obviously, Wilshire is doing great, so I don't even need to ask about him." Taking a sip of his straight black, he said with concern, "and how's my boy, Layne?"

"He's doing okay. He actually went to visit Katy's family in Ohio, to take some of her personal items to them, and attend the funeral. Since the visit with her family, he seems to be in much better spirits," she said.

Lenny leaned in across the desk. "So, what is it, Sara? Why are you here? What's wrong?"

Placing her hands on her temples, Sara rubbed them and squinted her eyes. "I'm sorry, Lenny, I don't know how to tell you this, other than just to tell you straight up."

With his curiosity now peaking, he leaned further in, and said, "Go on."

Sara took a deep sigh, and exhaled quickly. "When you were on your trip to Mexico, something happened. Had you been here, you would have known because it was temporarily leaked out all over the press." She took another deep breath and continued, "Since you were not here, we decided to keep it from you, to protect you. Your sanity. Tessa's sanity. We had twenty four hour protection detail on the both of you."

Lenny leaned back in his chair, and steepled his fingers. In a calm and rationally demanding voice, he asked, "What happened, Sara? Why the hell would we need twenty four hour protection detail?"

"Oh, God," she quaked. Her insides twisted, but she managed to spit the words out of her mouth. "To make a long and complicated story short, while you were away, Verde Senior donned an elaborate disguise, complete with falsified identification, and posed as Bobby Thorne's lawyer... They're gone, Lenny.

There gone, and we don't know where they are. They
could be out of state. Hell, they could be out of the
country, for that matter. That's why I'm here. We want
you on the case, Lenny. Not in an official capacity, of
course, but we want you. All of my resources would be
at your disposal." Sara sat there searching Lenny's
eyes for something. Anything would be good right
about now. Even anger. He didn't elicit any emotion at
the news.

Reaching into his pocket, he unwrapped and popped
a stick of Wrigley's into his mouth and chewed with
slow intention. Staring at Sara, he mulled everything
she said, over in his brain, before he spoke.

"Please say something," Sara begged. The stone look
he had on his face was more frightening than giving
him the actual news.

Lenny intertwined his fingers, and laid his hands on
his desk. His heart started to beat a little faster. He
couldn't tell if it was due to anger, disappointment, or
the impending excitement of the thrill of the chase. He
had caught both of the bastards before, so he could do
it again. And for round two, he wouldn't be bound by
all of the bureaucratic red tape. Ding. Ding. He was
ready to step into the ring, once again. "I have to speak
to the Missus first, but if it's all clear with her, when
do we start?

###

I hope you enjoyed reading "A Killer's Game," as much as I enjoyed writing it! BOLO (be on the look out) for the next Detective Lenny Shane Novel, "Killer Chase," coming soon! Keep reading for a sneak peak!

Connect with me on Face book @:
https://www.facebook.com/pages/Amy-Andrews/744581912249923?ref=hl

Thanks!
-Amy Andrews

COMING SOON…

# Killer Chase
## A Detective Lenny Shane Novel

## Amy Andrews

# CHAPTER ONE

"ARE you fucking serious," Tessa said, as her perfectly arched, sandy blonde brows shot up, just as much as her voice did. "Is that why Lieutenant Whitten came in to see you?" Standing there, with her hands splayed on the desk, she leaned in, impatiently waiting for an answer, while playing a drumming tune with her fingers.

Lenny Shane was a seasoned, but retired Homicide Detective, turned Private Investigator. In his days as a Detective, he had encountered some hairy situations, but he wasn't quite sure if any of them were as nerve racking as this. He leaned back in his desk chair, to cower away from the glare, and looming presence of his 5'2" wife, who was maybe 5"4" with the black designer boots she was currently wearing. He was a tough guy, but he would be the laughing stock of his former colleagues if his tombstone read, "death by stiletto," and with what he was asking, he was walking that thin line.

Shaking her head, her long blonde hair swished across her back as she said, "You are well aware that one of them tried to kill me. You remember that, right?"

Cupping his white mug in both hands, Lenny took a swallow of his black java, to let her bomb diffuse a bit before answering her. Setting the mug down on his cherry wood desk, he looked into her steel blue gaze. "Of course, I remember. How could I forget the day I came so close to losing the reason I live and breathe everyday? To tell you the truth, Tessa, I remember all too well, which is exactly why we need to do this. And yes, that is the main reason why Sara came to see me."

Throwing her hands in the air, Tessa said, "Why would she come to see you, Lenny?" Tessa's heels clicked across the floor as she started to pace. "You're not on the force anymore. You retired so we could get away from all of that….She stopped and turned towards him with a fury boiling in her eyes. "When I suggested you become a PI, *this* is not the type of case I had in mind, to occupy your time. *Our* time."

Tessa looked at him inquisitively, as he daringly continued. "Look, they have both escaped and eluded law enforcement, right under their noses. They could be anywhere by now. If they're out of this jurisdiction, there isn't much local law enforcement can do. Their hands are tied. At this point, it's in the hands of the Feds. Me? I'm no longer bound by the rules and red tape, Tessa. I played a major part in apprehending both Robert Verde Jr., and Sr. during my career as a Detective. And Junior, he had a personal vengeance vendetta against me, which is why you were in danger. Maybe he's over it, maybe he's not…but I can't take that chance, Tessa. I can't live everyday looking over

208        AMY ANDREWS

our shoulders. You and I were both the prey last time…this time, I prefer to be the hunter." Lenny consciously decided to omit the part where his former partner threatened to make sure the job got finished if there were a next time. Tessa didn't need to know that.

Tessa stood and tucked her hair behind one ear. Crossing her arms, she sighed heavily and whispered, "I suppose you're right."

Feeling pretty confident that it was safe, Lenny came out from around his desk, and cautiously approached her. Placing his hands on both of her shoulders he said, "Come again?"

Rolling her eyes, she said with pouting lips, "I said, I suppose you're right," Being almost a foot shorter than him didn't stop her from poking him in the chest. "But don't get too used to it, Mister," she warned him.

Smirking, Lenny kissed her on the forehead. "Don't worry Dear, I won't. So," he piped up as he headed towards the large dry erase board mounted on his office wall, "Lieutenant Whitten has enlisted our help. We will be given all the resources that are at her disposal, should we need them." Picking up the black marker, Lenny scribbled the names "Robert Verde Jr. / Bobby Thorne ?," and directly underneath that, "Robert Verde Sr.? " Turning towards Tessa, he gauged her face to see her reaction to seeing the name of one of the father/son duo sociopath killers. "Bobby Thorne," as they knew him, was an alias that "Robert Verde Jr." went by, and they knew him as. He was one of the most dangerous types…patient and cunning. He had actually killed a man to assume his identity. Living a lie for over five years, he was Detective Bobby Thorne, Lenny's Homicide partner on the force. All of this just to get close to Lenny to enact his plan of revenge for Lenny's role in putting his Father, Robert Verde Sr. away. Albeit, his plan included putting Tessa through a night of living hell.

Tessa narrowed her eyes, and straightened her spine.

Staring past Lenny, directly to the names on the board, she spoke without so much as a hint of fear in her voice. "Well, what are we waiting for then? Let's go nail the son of a bitches."

Lenny's chocolate eyes widened, and a smile settled on his lips. "Whoa there, girl," he chuckled. "First thing I need you to do is to go home and get packed. We need to be able to head out at a moment's notice. Bring all of your camera equipment, and don't forget to pack the long lenses.

Not sure how long we'll be on the road, so what I need you to do is to go get prepared for it. I'll be right behind you. I need to get some things around here," he said, signaling around the office. By "things," he meant surveillance equipment, guns, and ammunition, that he kept locked up in the office safe, but those were the details.

"So, I'll meet you back here in an hour or two," she said, as she strode out of the office.

# CHAPTER TWO

ROBERT Verde's hand started to cramp, as he tightened his grip around her throat. "Shh, shh, shh," he hushed her. "Just go to sleep, and it will all be over," he whispered to her, as he caressed her face.

Bobby Jr. stood there watching his Father drain the life out of yet another innocent young girl. Over the past month, he came to realize that killing was like a drug to his Father. He didn't just want to do it...he *needed* to do it. They were both on the run, and , as an ex homicide detective, he knew that leaving a trail of dead bodies wasn't exactly the way to keep a low profile. As the girl looked at him from across the room with begging eyes, his pulse started to race, and his eyes darted to the floor. No matter how much he tried to block it out, he could still hear the choking sounds escaping her mouth, as she desperately tried to claw his Father's hands from around her delicate neck. Yes, he himself had killed innocents before, but it always served a purpose, that had been fueled by revenge. Now that he had gained his Father back into his life, he wasn't quite so sure if his past actions weren't a mistake. He had hated his ex partner, Detective Lenny Shane for taking his Father away from him as a child, but sometimes in life, you think you know what's good for you, but you don't. Sometimes, you think you want something, and will do anything to get it, but once you've gained it, it doesn't turn out to be everything you thought it would be. Bobby didn't want her to have to die, but he also didn't want to disobey his Father, so he just stood there, as though his feet were cemented to the floor, gripping the sweet smelling bouquet of heather tighter and tighter. It was like he was a child, all over again, seeking his Father's love and approval.

Robert Sr. felt a release of adrenaline surge through him at the moment the last bit of life flickered out of the girl's eyes. He was never a drug user, but assumed the rush must be the same kind of fix. It was addictive.

Releasing his grip, the girl slumped to the floor. "Phew," he said, wiping off his sweaty brow with his forearm. He and Bobby locked eyes. "Now, that's a workout, son. She was a real bitch, that one." Reaching into his shirt pocket, he pulled out a Marlboro. "I need a smoke after that. Why don't you be a good Son, and clean up after your old man. After all, we just got back together again. You don't want to be torn apart again, do you Bobby? "

Unable to form any words, Bobby didn't say a word, so he just nodded his head., as his Father walked past him, and out the back door into the night air.

Verde finished his smoke, and was careful not to dispose of the butt. Instead, he snuffed it out, and placed it in his jeans pocket. He knew the cops couldn't discern anything from the ashes, so he didn't really care about them. Besides, by time they arrived, the wind would have scattered them through the city anyway, and he and his Son would be long gone by then.

Returning inside, Verde's eyes watered as he was hit with the caustic smell of bleach. Bobby had wiped down all of the walls, the floor, and the door with a bucket of it diluted with warm water. He smiled in appreciation at how well Bobby took care of his prizes. The girl was lying on her back, atop the break room table of the Circle K gas station,, with her hands gently clasping the bouquet of heather that he had given to Bobby to hold. He had even taken the time to close the girl's eyes. She looked peaceful and lovely. Just the same as she did when living. All except for the purplish bruising around her neck.

Satisfied that there were no traces of them ever being there, they grabbed their plastic bag of money, and helped themselves to a couple of snacks for the road. Robert stopped and turned around before walking out the door. He strode over to a large plastic bin, and plucked out a bouquet of pink carnations. Deeply inhaling the sweet scent, he smiled as he walked through the dimly lit lot towards the eighteen wheeler, where Bobby was already sitting behind the wheel, with the engine roaring.

Bobby felt his gut wrench at the sight of the bouquet, as his Father hopped into the passenger's seat, and slammed the door shut. He and his Father had been on the road for a month now, and it had become a predictable and reoccurring cycle. He no longer liked flowers, because when he saw his Father with some, he knew what it meant. It meant that someone was going to die. He didn't know why, but his Father always left the girls with a bouquet. Kind of like his signature, or calling card, he supposed. As of right now, he didn't know who was going to be so unfortunate, and he didn't know where. It all depended on where the road would take them. Even though he took no part in any of the murders, he felt a huge weight of responsibility and guilt for their deaths, because he was driving. He felt like he was an Angel of Death, leading the Devil. It would simply be a matter of being the right girl, at the wrong place, at the right time. It was a weighted feeling that had been building, and he just couldn't shake it, no matter how hard he tried.

ABOUT THE AUTHOR

Amy Andrews was born in Bowling Green, Ohio. In 1989, her family relocated to Southwest Florida, where she still resides. She enjoys the sunshine, surf, and sand, with her Husband, Son, and two rescue cats.

32576121R00136

Made in the USA
Charleston, SC
21 August 2014